Sin City Wolf

HUNT

JANUARY BAIN

Hunt
ISBN # 978-1-83943-741-0
©Copyright January Bain 2021
Cover Art by Claire Siemaszkiewicz ©Copyright September 2021
Interior text design by Claire Siemaszkiewicz
Totally Bound Publishing

HUNT

Dedication

Thank you, dear reader,
for coming along for the adventure.
Special thanks to Rebecca Baker Fairfax for
making my stories shine and
to the entire Totally Bound crew for all they do.
And, of course, to the light of my life, my
husband Don, thank you can never be enough.

Chapter One

Maximus

"Dearly beloved, we are gathered here today…"

Maximus vibrated with excessive energy, droning out the minister. Standing there like a stuffed turkey in his dove-gray morning coat and tails, waiting for his brother and mate to conclude the official ceremony, all he could think was *sign the damn contract already*. The sooner he got out of this godawful monkey suit and had an extended run in the clear, crisp desert air, the better.

He stretched his neck under the stiff white collar. There wasn't much call for such attire in the sacred halls of a dusty library, researching ancient writings, seeking clues to the whereabouts of sacred objects, in particular the House of Luceres' holiest of grails, the Lupus Sanguis Chalice. Just thinking of laying his hands on the priceless item made his pulse quicken.

Lives spent in the higher halls of learning was a calling he and his twin Alessandro were well suited to. He didn't want the unenviable job of being CEO of a string of worldwide casinos, like the ones his soon-to-be married brother reigned over, though he admired how his sibling managed the position with such style and grace.

But even Cristaldo had to release his wolf on occasion, to manage his beast effectively. Maximus hid a grin at the reminder of how off-the-rails his alpha sibling had become when he'd first met up with the lovely, all-too-human Everly. He'd nearly lost it, according to their brother Lucius — Cristaldo's twin — who took great glee in reminding everyone of the fact.

"And do you, Everly Joy Affini, take this man, Cristaldo Maximus Luceres, to be your lawfully wedded husband, until you are reborn?"

"I do."

The words sounded so final, albeit quite accurate, and were accompanied by a few notes of surprise from amongst the human wedding guests. They'd have been even more shocked if they understood what it *truly* meant — that once mated werewolves died after finding their Forever Mate, they reincarnated and came back and searched until they found each other. All they needed was a plan to meet up again, although the fragrance of their mate and the call of lust it created seemed to be sufficient in most cases. It was a fascinating world to be part of, one that would shock human sensibilities to their foundations. *Reason why we have to live in secret among them. Pack rule number one.*

"And do you, Cristaldo Maximus Luceres, take this woman, Everly Joy Affini, to be your lawfully wedded wife, until you are both reborn?"

"I do."

His brother raised his mate's veil and the look of adoration and love so clear in his eyes made Maximus glance away. Sly, sitting in the first row of pews as acting majordomo of the House of Luceres, let out a loud sob, his kindly face creased with contentment as he pressed a snowy-white handkerchief to his mouth.

A sense of need and envy stirred deep inside Maximus, its rawness taking him by surprise. *What is this?* He ran a finger between his shirt collar and his neck in an effort to loosen it. Taking a deep breath, he forced himself to remain still and see the final part of the ceremony to its expected conclusion. His twin Alessandro stirred at his side, apparently needing a deep breath of his own. The church was too hot and too stifling by half.

He held on, encouraged by a vision in his mind's eye of the pair of them racing across the desert floor, the crescent moon overhead lighting the way. He couldn't even begin to think of him and Alessandro finding their Forever Mate, though she haunted their dreams on occasion. *The one who will love us both. Does she even exist?*

His mind revisited an intoxicating scent he'd experienced for a couple of brief seconds a few months back while visiting their holdings in Milan. *Who was that female?* The fragrance had vanished before he could track her, an annoyance that still plagued him.

"You may now kiss your bride." The gleam in the minister's eyes expressed his understanding of who they were and the importance of the pair he was joining together for all eternity. Of course — he was their father, Cesare, home with their mother, Sophia, from traveling abroad. Their entire extended community was in attendance, from all corners of the globe. More than two hundred in total from their side of the family alone sat patiently, and some — mostly the male attendees — *impatiently* in the pews.

"I have to get out of here."

"Soon, bro. There's time between the ceremony and the reception for a good run."

The clock began to tick ever louder in his head. If it were just supernatural beings present, he could have got away with leaving before the bride and groom made their way down the aisle to be greeted by well-wishers and rice. But humans were a different matter.

By the time his father had finished his blessing of the newly married pair and the documents were signed, his entire body felt about to vanish into one of the multiverses where they became wolves...and this time not come back. *Run forever free on the other side.*

Not that he had caught more than a glimpse of that special dimension in his decades plus of shifting. He'd studied the phenomenon of course, understanding that in physics energy was never lost and that werewolves became altered at the quantum level due to their special DNA.

He imagined explaining *that* to a physics professor at the Sapienza in Rome where he and his twin were currently scholars in residence. But understanding it and preventing it were two different things. He had no more control at times than a chameleon that changed color in a new environment, especially when the full moon called.

A new energy in the air woke him from his musings. The agony was over and everyone was moving, following the newly married pair down the red carpet to the open doorway. He took a big breath of fresh air into his starved lungs outside the church doors, watching the crowd mill about, vying for their chance to speak to the happy couple.

"Let's nab the 'copter before anyone else gets the same idea," Maximus said, jerking off his black tie and thrusting it into his jacket pocket. Undoing a few buttons on his white shirt front, his muscles tight with the urgent need to release the pent-up strain of the past few days, he thumped his twin on the back. Alessandro stood beside him on the church steps, his expression calm. He'd always been the more patient one, from the moment of birth when he'd let his twin exit first. "Let's go."

Less than ten minutes later, they were buckling themselves into the seats of the helicopter. It was gassed and ready, perched like a sleek beast on the roof of the Glitter Palace casino.

Maximus took over the controls and the rush of lift from the powerful engine quickly soared them high above the desert floor. He set course for the vast desert property the pack also owned near Sin City. Not that his twin was any less proficient, but Alessandro tended to let him lead, a situation that alleviated brotherly rivalries…most of the time.

"Perhaps we'll be next," Alessandro mused, his expression distant when Maximus glanced over at him.

He snorted at the idea while keeping a close eye on the numerous gauges that lined the cockpit, glancing out through the side window for the landing pad. "Not likely, bro. Not many women want two men in their bed. At least, not many that will admit it. Besides, she'll like me best once I show her my considerable assets." He added a wolfish grin for good measure, wanting to ensure his twin didn't experience the slump that the festivities tended to bring to unmated pack members.

"It's not what you have, bro, it's knowing how to use it. And it's not all about the cock. Your tongue can be mightier. And my talent in that direction is legendary."

The reply surprised him. This mate they spoke of was a fantasy, and yet here was his brother testing him.

"When she takes my knot, it'll be all over but the fat lady singing."

Alessandro remained quiet while Maximus set down the whirlybird on the pad and killed the motor. Unbuckling his harness, Maximus reminded them why they were there. "Mate or no mate, time to hunt."

"Oh yeah, you're on."

They both jumped to the ground and began shedding their clothing as if they were on fire. When Alessandro was naked, his warrior body revealed in all its glory in the moonlight, from his wide chest to his muscled abs to his strong thighs, Maximus knew he was seeing a mirror image of himself. A very satisfying image. They also had in common thick dark hair that refused to be tamed and cocks that wouldn't quit.

But now was the time to be free. Anticipation took over and he embraced the change. In seconds, he was through the portal that glinted with sparks of light when he entered it, every cell of his body shifting to a new form, before he was thrown back through again.

Changed. To a wolf.

He stretched and blinked, his keen senses honed to a deadly sharpness. He lifted his muzzle to catch the faint breeze, testing, hungry for distraction. The arid landscape was enhanced with his new vision, mutated to an array of shades unknown to the human eye. Subtle hues of blacks, browns and grays. Movements of tiny creatures caught his attention before he caught the scent of a big horn sheep.

This way.

He led the chase, his big paws closing the distance in leaps and bounds. It was good to be wolf. So good that he allowed himself the luxury of a resounding howl of wolf song, meant to tighten the senses of all creatures of the desert.

"You'll frighten our prey away."

He didn't like the reminder. Sure, he was spontaneous at times, but it beat taking too long to make a decision—one of Alessandro's characteristics that could bite them in the ass one day if he hesitated at the wrong moment.

"There will be lots of others, bro. Stand down."

He used his powerful body to give his sibling a solid nudge on the upper shoulder. Alessandro hit back, harder than he had.

"Bring it on." Sibling rivalry helped keep them in top physical form and he was more than ready for the challenge.

Their hard bodies twisted and slammed together with a loud resounding *thud*, both of them hitting the hard-packed sand as one snarling, swirling mass of limbs and fur. He fought hard, looking for an opening. All he needed was a slight pause in the action where he could take his brother down. *Make him submit.* Seconds ticked by as each sought the advantage, strutting and sending out telepathic taunts.

"I have the bigger knot."

"I have the most talented tongue."

The wrestling match, fueled by the week's limiting formal events, continued unabated for far longer than usual. Neither of them could win without doing the other harm. And that was not the point. But still they fought, past the time they should have stopped. *The lust for a mate.* That was at the base of this primal drive. Maximus sensed this even as he couldn't stop himself from asserting his alpha pride over his brother's.

His flanks shuddering with exhaustion, he locked his jaws onto the back of Alessandro's neck to get him under control.

A long loud growl of warning caused him to break his hold in an instant. He tensed and peered into the darkness, legs bracing for combat with the intruder. Alessandro stood at his side, prepared as well to rise to the challenge. Over there, near a Joshua tree, a gleam of bright blue pin points—a third wolf. And behind him, other dark shadows appeared, eyes shining in the darkness, a solid line of danger.

"Recognize any of them?" Alessandro asked.

Maximus bristled, growling a warning deep inside his massive chest. The line of gray wolves descended closer toward the brothers, their huge paws closing the gap between them in a matter of seconds.

"Stand down. We need your help."

Raising his muzzle to test the air, he recognized the scent of pack visiting for the wedding.

"What do you want?"

"We have a wolf-bit female. She's dying. We come to implore you to redouble your efforts to find the chalice. To offer our help."

He understood now which cousins he and Alessandro faced. The group from Los Angeles that normally kept to themselves, preferring to keep apart from the Vegas pack.

"We work alone." No one wanted the artifact as badly as he and Alessandro. Not after what had happened—a devastating event that had torn them apart and was never to be spoken of again.

Low growls from the wolves opposite him followed his words, making the ruff bristle on his neck.

"We will share what we know." Alessandro, ever the peacemaker, reassured the other pack.

"Good." The largest of the wolves gave a nod of his huge head. *"It's too late for our female, but others may be*

saved. Come and see her. Tonight. Then you will know how bad it is."

Yes, he knew all too well how bad it could be. A terrible sense of foreboding, like a living, evil presence that sucked up all the oxygen in the air, placed a cold hand on his heart. Fear of the worst thing that could happen.

The loss of a true mate can end a wolf...and turn them into a creature of death and destruction.

Chapter Two

Trinity

Trinity Wells laid the four of spades atop the ace and six of clubs, adopting an innocent and surprised expression. The male dealer frowned, unhappy that she'd beaten him yet again. All a card counter required was an eidetic memory and a family screaming at her to bring home the goods and they, too, would win as many hands of blackjack as humanly possible.

Maybe they can also earn a nickname. Not that *The Chameleon* was negative, more like appropriate considering the many appearances of Trinity, all devised from a one single suitcase stuffed with useful disguises. But then wasn't everyone something of a chameleon, as John Locke suggested in *Some Thoughts Concerning Education*? *We take our hue and the color of our moral character from those who are around us.*

There was nothing Trinity enjoyed more than a wise quote. She sprinkled her life and her research notes with them, trying to make sense of the world and the people in inhabiting it, especially her family. Her stomach tightened with thoughts of *that* complicated relationship. A childhood that had guilted her to the point she pretty much let them run amok over her needs. But what else was there to do?

Her parents had been there for her when no one else had been, had kept her from being driven crazy by her growing abilities when her brain couldn't seem to shut itself off, taunting her day and night with thoughts and ideas. Making peace with her abilities had not come easily and as a small child she'd been certain that men in white coats would come for her, haul her away and lock her up tight in some dismal prison. Her parents had saved her from that. Kept her safe. *And now I owe them big time.*

She gathered up her chips and, tossing the dealer one, turned to make her escape. *Never get greedy and take too many hands in any one place.* Though her luck was better than average at the Glitter Palace — always a plus no matter how brilliant one was at counting cards — there was no point in pushing it.

"Miss, you need to come with us," a security guard said, his face inscrutable, laying his hand with authority on her shoulder. He was a sturdy guy with wide shoulders and a well practiced ready-for-any-kind-of-action look.

"I think not." She shook her head for emphasis, the dark wig swaying over her shoulders keeping her face partially hidden. She watched him intently through her tinted glasses perched on her larger-than-real-life nose. It wasn't bad enough that she seemed to be constantly dealing with odd, random thoughts these days that came out of nowhere, now she had to deal with this situation? "I've done nothing wrong and I wouldn't go off with a stranger for anything. How do I know you are who you say you are?"

"You've been flagged. It will go easier for you if you just come along quietly."

"And if I chose to make a ruckus? Alert others to my being abducted by a complete stranger? Say...I scream about how you're hurting me or touched me inappropriately?" It was the last thing she wanted to do, draw attention to herself, but she'd do anything to get away with the money. It was that or suffer guilt for not helping her parents out enough.

He flushed, his dark eyes smoldering with anger. "We are a family establishment—no one would dare touch you inappropriately. Plus, the eye in the sky records everything, so your complaints will not hold water."

"Yes, but by the time that's all figured out, think of the bad publicity." She got up and pulled free of the man, tucking the purse holding the chips under her arm. "I'm walking out of here and I won't be back. Good enough?"

Her words had affected the man. He hesitated, then made his offer. "If you turn over your winnings, it will be."

"Not going to happen, buddy!" She grabbed a tighter hold of her purse. She needed the winnings to get the monkey off her back, let her begin her new job as a TA to a professor at the Sapienza in peace. It was such a coup gaining that position. And it might lead to other teaching opportunities which would ultimately create a better future, *sans* gambling. At least, that was her secret hope.

She strode away on the high-heeled boots she'd donned earlier, the heels clicking officiously on the marble floor. The man continued to hound her, jogging alongside her, trying to head her off.

"Enough of this shit!" She had no choice now.

She screamed once. Loud and piercing. Everyone around her froze, some dropping to the floor, looking for the active shooter. Then she was off and running, through the front doors of the casino before anyone— especially the security guard—had a chance to stop her. Unfortunately, she barrelled right into a huge man coming into the hotel, hitting him with such brute force she was stopped dead in her tracks, dropping the precious bag of chips. The purse burst open, spilling its contents.

"Now look what you've done!" she exclaimed, getting onto her knees to retrieve the multi-colored disks.

It took a few seconds before she realized the man was actually helping to pick up her belongings. When he handed her a huge handful of casino chips and a tube of lipstick, she was startled enough to check out who was assisting her.

One of the owners. She recognized him from photos she'd seen during her recognizance mission of researching the casino. And strangely enough, his bio said he was from the same university that she attended in Rome, though they'd never met. She ducked her head and scrambled to finish the job. Of all the people to run into, one of the Luceres twins was last on the list of probable people she wanted to have this encounter with. Her anxiety jacked up just thinking of what could occur if he discovered who she was.

"Thanks." She thrust the last of the items in the purse, held it closed to keep it from spilling again and backed away, preparing to run.

"Hold on. Don't you want to cash those in?" His dark presence loomed over her. All the Luceres men were so damn big and strong. She couldn't help herself from wondering if the theme maybe carried over to the bedroom?

"No time now. I'll be back." *For heaven's sake, just let this go.* She was so close to getting away that she could taste freedom in the back of her throat. She checked out the traffic. *Yes.*

"I think you'd better do it now." The words sounded cold, steeled by a will that brooked no refusal. It sent a frisson of heat down her spine, hijacking something deep inside her. This was a man who knew who he was and would take what he wanted without quarter. She'd have to keep her guard up. *Way up.* It didn't help that he was surveying her with increasing interest or that her body responded to the unspoken proposition with keen interest of its own.

"Ah, sorry, I can't. Obligations, you understand." She was prepared to flee. This guy might be big, but he probably wasn't expecting a track star who would have gotten Olympic gold if she'd had the backing to continue her quest.

Of course, the security guard had to make himself known at that moment, hurrying up to them with a pissed-off expression. "Thank goodness you stopped her, Mr. Luceres. We've been wanting to nab this cheater. She just pulled a stunt that got everyone wired — screaming her fool head off."

"I'm not a cheater! Since when is it wrong to use your God-given gifts? So, I've got a brilliant memory. Wouldn't you use it to help your family? Keep them in groceries?"

"I think you got more in that purse than the cost of a month's groceries. Looks more like enough for ten families," Luceres said, firming his mouth into a straight line.

"I have a large family. And they need rent money, electric, water, school fees — "

He held up one large hand, his heavy gold cuff links gleaming in the overhead marquee lights shining down on the Vegas strip. He was dressed in what was obviously an expensive suit, his dress shirt glowing white against the black herringbone fabric and silver tie. "We'll settle it all inside, Miss…?"

"Miss Jones," she said without losing a beat. That was the fake name on the ID card she'd chosen for this trip.

He held out his hand, offering to shake hers. "Maximus Luceres."

She took it tentatively, pretending to capitulate, feeling his warmth zing her in all the right places. Damn, but the man let off a fine fragrance of hot cinnamon and danger. If things were different, she'd jump his bones in a New York minute. She tugged her fingers away when he held on a second too long.

He'd relaxed at the peace gesture, prepared to escort her back inside. When he turned his attention to the security guard to answer an urgent question, she whirled around and fled to the curb, jumping into the taxi she'd spotted earlier and slammed the door closed as Maximus turned to observe her, his expression a mask of outrage.

"Go!" she screamed at the driver. Thankfully, the woman had the wherewithal to floor the gas pedal and in a split second they were off, joining the traffic flow.

"Where to?" the driver asked, giving her an assessing look in the rear-view mirror.

"The Last Chance motel, on the outskirts."

"Are you sure? Kind of a seedy joint for a woman alone. And it looks like you won big. Just sayin'."

Obviously, the woman had observed the altercation.

"Yeah, I'm sure." She'd never waste precious funds on anything more than the rudimentary essentials. *Bed and a bath. At least the place is clean.*

Traffic and fancy marquees flowed by the window for a number of impressive blocks filled with towering hotel and casino complexes, before changing to smaller venues until finally petering out to the dribs and drabs of less-successful businesses. Past that was The Last Chance, living up to its name.

She paid the driver, leaning over the back seat into the front and adding a generous tip.

"Let's keep this between us. Okay?"

"My lips are sealed. How did you win the money anyway?" The middle-aged woman with the big Vegas hair chewed gum as she asked her question, smacking the wad with gusto. The faux-fruit of pink bubble gum saturated the cab, a not-unpleasant fragrance.

She tapped the side of the wig she couldn't wait to discard with a couple of stiffened fingers. "Card counting."

"I consider that fair. It's a gift, right? Not like those casinos can't afford it. They take, take, take. Time we took them for a change."

She liked the woman's philosophy. "Can be. Some gamblers practice it. Mine came naturally."

She hoped the woman wouldn't share her address with anyone at the Glitter Palace until she checked out. Would the casino go that far to hound her? She shrugged. *Maybe.* But she considered herself a fair judge of human character and she'd bet the woman wouldn't go behind her back to share her location.

"Thanks for the ride."

"Any time, hon."

She stepped out of the vehicle and, shouldering her purse, headed inside the motel.

One of the florescent lighting tubes overhead the lobby desk was strobing, about to give up the ghost, when she yanked open the heavy metal door. The desk clerk was nowhere to be seen. She stepped up to the desk and hit the bell provided. Its tinny sound jarred and she gritted her teeth.

"Evenin', Trinity," the night clerk said, coming through the curtain that separated the lobby from the office. The tall, lanky man, whose sallow skin looked as though it never felt the rays of the sun, greeted her with his usual shy smile.

"Hi, Jack. Any messages for me?" Her father seemed to enjoy the old-fashioned way of staying in touch. Everyone else just texted her, like the rest of the world.

"Not tonight. Say, did you hear about that tourist being bit by a wolf last night? Not more than a few blocks from here over on Waverly? You'd best be careful."

"I'm always careful, Jack. You know that." Should she check out? She trusted Jack. "You'd let me know if anyone came looking for me, right?"

He looked scandalized. "Is someone looking to do you harm? That's why I keep a shotgun under the counter." He leaned down and picked it up, careful to keep it pointed away from her. "Anyone comes for you, they'll be speaking to the business end of old Bessie."

"Thanks, but a phone call to alert me will do."

"Easily taken care of. But I'll keep old Bessie ready just in case." He gave the shotgun a loving pat and placed it back under the counter.

"Catch you later." She turned and went back outside, headed for her room at the far end. The one-storey motel gave off the desperation vibes that it wanted to sink even farther into the desert sand than it already had. *Embarrassed at its comedown from former glory, no doubt.* One day this would all be gone, all the flash of Vegas, but at least not in her lifetime and that was all the time she needed.

She hoped eighty-plus years would be enough to make her mark on the world and accomplish all her hopes and dreams—only after she escaped her background, which constantly threatened to derail her plans. How much money would that take? Could she ever pay off the guilt debt from being such a problem to her parents? She'd driven her father to drink and her mother to exhaustion. And all due to their worry over her 'talents' exposing the family to harm if she was ever allowed free rein—she could have started fires, or done something equally bad, with her volatile nature.

She stopped at the vending machine that offered snacks and drinks then scrambled around in her bag for change, her mind still distracted with thoughts of the uncomfortable relationship with her family. Out of the darkness, something huge and dark lunged at her. It grabbed hold of her arm with its wicked teeth that gleamed yellow in the dim light, its eyes a strange unworldly blue. The creature bit down on her forearm.

Hard.

She screamed and swung at it with her purse, hitting at it with all she had, the chips once more flying and spilling out onto the sidewalk. The animal backed off, gazing at her with those unholy eyes, before it turned and loped away. She knew it could have done her more harm.

Why didn't it? Those eyes seemed to hold an intelligence that didn't fit any animal she'd ever seen. But with blood streaming off her arm and people coming outside alerted by her shouting, she had no time to think about it. She needed to pick up her winnings and get the hell out of there...before it was too late.

Chapter Three

Alessandro

Three weeks later Alessandro Luceres crept up the steep stone steps of Rocco Maggiore Castle, listening intently. The ancient fortress was built on a rocky promontory, the tower jutting out over the valley below. The image of a great battle filled his mind. It had been between a priest and a suspected werewolf, and the man of God had struck down the beast with a silver crucifix, killing him on the spot. It was a legend not even the townspeople knew of as the priest had also died soon after of his injuries, never to regain consciousness. Their spirits lingered still, linked by mortal combat. He crossed himself, offering a whispered prayer of release in Italian, "*Possa la vostra anima trovare rifugio e guarigione in Cielo.*"

"I doubt their souls will ever find refuge and healing in heaven, brother," Maximus said. His twin spared him a backward glance as he climbed the steps two at a time. With their mind connection, he'd caught a glimpse of what Maximus had planned for after the job, which explained his hurried actions. He had his sights focused on a certain female.

"If we find it, there will be more than enough healing to go around," Alessandro mused. No drawing existed of the Lupus Sanguis Chalice they were hunting. With it made from the bone and blood of the original wolf, its legendary status had kept a handful of treasure hunters fascinated for centuries, the quest handed down from father to son. Could it really do what it was purported to do? Ease the transformation of human to wolf? If so, the House of Luceres stood on the threshold of a brand-new era, unlike any that had come before. Finally, their numbers could grow, giving them increased strength in the modern world...if care was taken in the process.

"Where's the faith, brother? It could very well be here. The chalice has to be somewhere, right?"

Maximus had always had an excess of confidence. *Some might call it hubris.* Perhaps his legendary skills at anything he pursued was reason enough. "We can't be certain. Maybe it was never meant to be found. It will change things—maybe too much. If it ever fell into the wrong hands, think of what might happen?"

Alessandro shivered, imagining a vast horde of werewolves being created and taking over the world. As it stood now, few humans survived a werewolf bite. The majority of the Luceres numbers were from an ancient bloodline from the founding of Rome, and they were blessed with the DNA of the original wolf, guaranteeing a smooth change. They still found one of their original number on occasion, like his alpha and brother's Forever Mate, Everly Affini. But it happened so rarely now that too many males were without their mate. And moon sickness lurked for those unable to forge a permanent bond.

"Shush, I hear something."

A slight furtive scratching echoed in the vaulted staircase. Maximus pointed ahead. *In the tower. Human.* A faint hint of wolf gave him pause. What was this?

Alessandro nodded, though the mix of odors his brother thought-mentioned troubled him. Adjusting his pack, he stealthily climbed the final few steps. Rounding a corner, he caught a glimpse of the culprit down on her hands and knees, her shapely ass pointed in their direction. The woman was digging with a trowel at the corner stone marked with a crude pentagram symbol. Bricks and mortal lay crumbled by her side, heaped in a small pile. A stiff breeze gaining entrance through the doorway that led to the balcony installed for tourist caused the white dust to skitter across the stone floor.

He shed his backpack and hurried to her side. Before he could get to her, Maximus had her in a tight grip, her arms pinned behind her back, his expression fueled by anger.

"What do you think you're doing?" his brother asked, his voice edged by steel.

"Let me go," she said, struggling to pull away.

"Not until you tell me what you're after."

"Same thing as you, I imagine. The wolf blood chalice." Her defiant look challenged them to say any different.

"Who are you?" Alessandro asked. He felt the sudden heat of interest coursing through his brother's bloodstream. His own wolf took notice at the exact same second, doubling the lust that threatened to overcome both of them. *What is this?*

She chewed at her lips, a clouded look in her light blue eyes. Some slight noises of a vehicle's straining motor being driven up the winding route to the castle meant this had to be speeded up.

Maximus took a deep breath, his expression concerned. *"I just realized I know who she is. She was in disguise — I caught her counting cards in Vegas. But something's different about her. Something in her eyes... Be careful, bro. The lust may be attributed to the call of the siren, a ruse to cover her real intentions. Or someone may have control of her. I can't tell yet. And you know what that means."*

"I'm Trinity Wells, a grad student at the Sapienza. And newly hired assistant to the professor," Trinity said with a defiant shake of her head. "And I got here first, so I have dibs on the artifact. It's mine by right."

"Not bloody likely, *tesoro*. My family's got prior claim by a couple of millennia," Maximus said with feigned contempt. In reality, Alessandro could read his brother's eager interest in having her in their bed under his objections. *She smells like heaven under that slight scent of wolf.*

"How's that even possible?" She frowned, pursing her lips into a bow. And beautiful lips they were. Were they as soft and plush as they appeared? He had a strong impulse to test his theory.

"The less you know the better. Now, we'll finish this up and be on our way. The guard will be on rounds shortly. I'd prefer to avoid him."

"Frightened of a middle-aged guard?" she scoffed at his brother. Maximus still had a grip on her and she tried to pull away from him with a violent jerk of her body. She didn't succeed.

He gave Alessandro a significant look. *"We have to take her with us. Find out why she knows of the chalice and why she smells of wolf. We have to get to the bottom of this."*

"She knows nothing. Probably just wanted the artifact for the university's collection."

"But she knows what it's for and she knows we were here. She will talk, trust me. Better we have her mind wiped. Besides, she took us for fools counting cards at our casino. She's up to something and I want to know what it is. And who else knows of the existence of the chalice if she's working for someone."

Alessandro nodded. He wouldn't object to having this particular female around longer. He picked up the abandoned trowel, digging out the remaining mortar and bricks. He made quick work of it, and in a short period exposed the metal edges of a small iron chest. Pulling the item out of the hole it had obviously spent hundreds of years buried in, he yanked the lid off. He let out a hiss of disgust.

"Damn it, just another clue."

He pulled out the thick rolled-up parchment, smoothed it out, and read the verse aloud, automatically translating the faded, beautifully inscribed words from Italian to English.

"Those that seek the mother's blessing of blood and bone,

Shall find it hidden far from here in coldest depths of ice and stone.

In newer worlds, the tracks appear,

Upon a land of midnight sun,

The highest point of land is near, and shall reveal when all is clear."

Maximus gave a disgusted shake of his head. "I'm surprised we haven't found one warning about *'when the wolfbane blooms and the Autumn moon is bright'.*"

"Off by a few centuries, bro. Besides, isn't the first part about being pure of heart?"

His brother gave a snort. "Yeah, I'm about as pure of heart as — well, never mind. How many clues is this already? It's beginning to feel like we've been on nothing but a wild-goose chase."

"What do you think the new clue means?"

"Land of the midnight sun? Sounds like Alaska. Not too big a haystack."

"Looks like. Okay, I'll pack this away and we'll get out of here." Alessandro jumped to his feet, his body charged with adrenaline. He'd thought this might be the time all was revealed. But no precious seconds to waste, if they planned to leave by a different route than they had arrived and achieve a clean getaway.

"That's mine!" Trinity made a sudden lunge for the parchment, nearly escaping the hold Maximus had on her. She had a desperation look about her that gave him pause. Her wild eyes gave her a look of obsession, far too intense by half. His brother was right. Something was up with her, more than then could be accounted for in the seething lust that electrified the air between them. "I have to have that. Give it to me!"

Alessandro avoided her easily and tucked the paper away inside his jacket, zipping it up tight. "We need it more."

"To the balcony," Maximus said. They tugged Trinity along with them, her protests kept to the bare minimum so as not to be overheard. But her shoes skidded across the stones worn smooth from centuries of use as she tried to dig her heels in. She was no match for their strength and the three of them were soon standing over the steep embankment and looking down at the darkened valley lurking hundreds of feet below. The setting sun added long shadows with the promise of darkness soon to cover their tracks.

"What are you doing?" Trinity asked.

"You've given us no choice. You have to come with us. What was your plan for escape, or didn't you think that far ahead?" he asked. They couldn't shift to wolves minus opposable thumbs to get away with the artifact they had hoped to acquire. Instead, they had decided on making use of their excellent hang-gliding skills.

"I intend to walk right out of here. Why should anyone suspect me? Besides, most men are easily led by their cocks." She gave them both a steely look. She obviously knew how turned on they all were.

Well, she was right there. If she grabbed his cock right now, no telling where that would lead. But her determination rang so oddly, like she was obsessed with obtaining the chalice. *Why?*

"Feminine wiles will only get you so far," Maximus warned.

While Maximus held on to her, Alessandro pulled out a harness shaped like a padded chair from his own backpack. They thrust her unceremoniously into it, then strapped her in tightly. Attaching himself behind her with a secure strap, he unfurled the nylon wing with the two guide wires that dangled down. The soft fabric billowed up and out above them. The strong winds tugged on the nylon, pulling them forward.

The small balcony wasn't large enough for both brothers to jump simultaneously, but Maximus was about ready, jumping into his own harness in the doorway while unfurrowing his own hang-gliding equipment. He waited to see if his brother's wing clipped in properly, then gave him the thumbs-up.

He ignored the continuing protests from Trinity, and releasing the handbrakes, stepped up to the ledge, giving in to the wind's desires. For a brief moment, they were plunging toward the earth before his chute caught an upward draft and raced up the ridge, jerking them above the treetops. Using the hand grips and weights to control his lateral movements, he slowly maneuvered them across the valley.

When he heard the satisfying whooshing sound of another chute catching the wind, he turned to catch his brother's wide grin from the sudden rush of the fall. The balcony behind them was still empty and meant that they'd gotten away cleanly.

He released the tension on his hand grips, allowing his wing to race down the valley, relishing the brief moment of total freedom. They'd soon be on solid ground and headed for the two-hour journey back to Rome. The fragrance of his captive washed over him from the stiff headwind blowing his way—an intoxicating scent of clean soap, hints of jasmine with an undertone of sweet female musk…but with the slight addition of a wolf. What was causing that?

But, more important, what to do about her? She was a big problem that had to be resolved soon. But thoughts of having her mind wiped made him pause. He didn't want her manhandled by a damned bloodsucker. The very idea made him want to punch one of the undead into oblivion. But she couldn't go around knowing of the priceless artifact's existence either. It put all wolves at risk, them included. And worse yet, it put her in danger, and neither he nor Maximus would allow that.

Chapter Four

Trinity

The stiff wind sucked the breath right out of her body as they flew through the dark. It tore at her braids, the pins she'd restrained them with no match for the breeze unravelling them. *Exhilarating but scary.* She nevertheless felt safe enough pressed against Alessandro's broad chest, the night sky above littered with stars seeming to guide their path across the valley. She deliberately chose not to look down. In fact, she'd do anything to keep her mind off the fact that the ground was rushing by hundreds of feet beneath them.

Why am I here? Not like I planned this heist out for weeks or that it's my normal MO. In fact, it had been just recently that the idea of snatching the artifact before Alessandro and Maximus had risen as a viable idea. Maybe she was coming down with something?

Her mind had been fuzzy of late, far too obsessed with getting to the chalice first, even with all her efforts to fight it. It was just now, with the wind rushing over her, that she realized just how out of it she had been. How powerless at times she had felt. Her arm began to ache where she'd been bitten and she absently rubbed at it.

"Bring it to us."

The words entered her mind unbidden and she shook her head violently, trying to dislodge the thought. A second later she wasn't certain she'd heard the command. Was it any of it real?

And why did the brothers want the chalice so badly anyway? She'd seen the look of supreme interest in their eyes when they'd thought she'd dug it up, and wished a man would look at her with half that excitement, though she had caught the heat with which Alessandro had stared at her. And she had to admit, her interest had been aroused. But it made no sense to feel such emotions over an old artifact reputed to be made of bone. Sure, it was old and worth some serious money, though it really belonged in a museum.

Maybe she could talk to them into it, the ones who wanted it so badly and had pushed her to find it. The ones who had demanded she keep their identify a secret. As if the legends about the Lupus Sanguis Chalice could ever be proven true. *Really. Does anyone believe anymore that a relic could help a human become a werewolf? Or that werewolves even exist? What century is this?*

"Steady. We're about to land."

She swallowed, the tug of the hand brakes engaging and jerking her backward tighter yet against Alessandro and making her aware of the fact that her hang-gliding partner was aroused. She wiggled her rear against him, more to tease after what he'd done to her than anything else, though it ended up arousing her too. Alessandro and his twin were fine male specimens. *Too handsome for their own good. Far too clever and rich.* The money didn't faze her overmuch—though her family might disagree—as she was far more interested in intellectual pursuits, but there was no denying the attraction. Or at least, until they'd pulled this stunt. Now she was ready to make them pay. *Full price.*

The land rushing up to greet them pushed everything else right out of her brain except thoughts of survival. Holding her breath, she closed her eyes as they landed near the treeline, certain she'd be lucky to only acquire a broken bone or two. But the landing was soft, barely jarring her, and she opened her eyes in surprise. *Of course, skilled at hang-gliding too.*

She heard Maximus land while his twin worked to remove her from the harness. Free to move around after a few seconds, she pushed the tangled lengths of hair back from her face, wishing she had a way of securing it, but all the pins had been lost during their flight. Drawing a deep steadying breath into her lungs, she scanned the area. *Which way to run?*

"Don't even think about it. We've got things to discuss," Alessandro said. It was fully dark now and she glanced at the forest. When he bent down to thrust the harness into the backpack, she made her move. In a burst of speed, she raced for the trees, her legs eating up the distance in seconds. If she could just make the other side of the thick grove, she'd be close to her vehicle and could make her escape.

Legs pumping, blood surging and pounding in her head, she ran full bore. The darkness swallowed her up immediately, the foliage great cover, but also great danger. *Please don't let me twist an ankle or strike my head on some tree limb.*

Footsteps pounded behind her, making her run all the faster. *Don't look back.* Just twenty-five feet ahead, she could see the opening that led onto the road where she'd parked an hour earlier. Her car's silver roof gleamed in the light of the overhead streetlamp, beckoning with promises of freedom.

Suddenly she was slammed to the ground. Not from behind, but from the front. How had that happened? *No way someone could have gotten past me in the dark.* No one could go that fast. But here she was on her back, with a huge body covering hers.

"Let me go!"

"Not on your life," Alessandro growled.

She took a deep breath, his clean scent of soap and musk filling her lungs with enticement. Something stirred in her, her belly tightening. He felt good, too good. His warmth invaded her, his long thighs and broad chest pushed against her in a way that made her mouth water. *No way.* This was not happening. *They just stole something from me and now I get turned on?*

"Get off me, you oaf!" She twisted and tried to shove him away. She might as well have been pushing at a huge boulder, for all the good it did.

"You'd better let me go or so help me..." She sputtered with anger, not sure how to back up the threat.

"Or you'll what?" He had the audacity to ask in a tone that implied he was unconcerned. Instead of letting her go, he lifted one of her errant locks of hair and rubbed it between his fingers.

"Just like the purest silk. Your shampoo hints at coconut and warm tropical breezes." He nuzzled her neck, making her all the more turned on—and angry for appearing weak.

"Big man to hold down a small woman."

He sprang off her immediately and hauled her to her feet, though he appeared a bit too smug. *No way he could know I was lusting after him, right?*

Maximus stood nearby, arms over his chest. His eyes glittered in the darkness. Did they just flash bright blue? But then a split second later they appeared normal and she shook her head. *Must have imagined it.*

"You're coming with us, the easy way or the hard way. Your choice, *tesoro*," Maximus said.

"I'm not your sweetheart, *stronzo*."

"Nice language. Where's the sugar-sweet little scholar now?"

"Enough. Let's get out of here. We need to make a new plan," Alessandro said.

"I'm not going with you. I've done nothing wrong. You have no right," she said. She stood her ground. Her ire was making her wrist hotter, and she absently scratched at it.

"No can do. You're coming with us." Maximus grabbed her and began to lead her away. Alessandro nabbed her other arm and she was sandwiched between them. All the air left her body at their combined touch. *Whoa.* Why was she suddenly on fire? Heat held her hostage as much as the brothers' physical restraints.

"Where are we going?" she asked, tripping along between them, not sure if she should be more afraid of them or herself for being so turned on by the intriguing pair of brothers.

Chapter Five

Maximus

"A place we can work out a plan on how to handle things with you," Alessandro said, answering the female's inquiry.

"I don't need to be handled!" the spitfire had the audacity to say.

"I think you do. Look at all the trouble you've caused so far. You've got a lot of explaining to do. Like what are you doing here for one? And why were you counting cards in my casino, then running off and not facing the music?" Maximus accused her.

He didn't need the distraction right now. *Too much at stake with the new clue to follow.* And this female, why was she attracting him and Alessandro anyway? She was human, and only half-Italian, which meant her bloodline couldn't possibly be an exact match for them. But even with that faint hint of wolf, her own fragrance was exhilarating, mesmerizing, and made him want to throw her down on the ground and ravish her senseless.

"I have every right to search for artifacts. As for my use of card counting, what do you want me to do? Ignore my gifts? Not going to happen, *stronzo!*"

Thankfully their black SUV appeared in the darkness, parked on the roadside. He wanted nothing more than to get the hell out of there.

"We'll discuss it later."

"Not my problem," she said, snapping her answer like she had a choice.

Alessandro pulled open the passenger door and Maximus pushed her inside, leaning over her to buckle the seatbelt securely then locked the door so she couldn't escape.

"So, where to?" his brother asked.

"I'm thinking the closest villa outside the city. No point in taking her back to Rome until we get to the bottom of things. Hell of a mess."

"Yeah, I know. But we can't hide her for long."

"We won't have to. Once we know what we need to know and have her mind wiped, she can leave. Unscathed."

"You know how I feel about that," Alessandro groaned. "Vampires are disgusting." He didn't want one of those cold suckers touching Trinity either, but what choice did they have? They couldn't have humans running around knowing about the priceless chalice and exposing their kind.

"We can't have her talking about this, so what do you suggest?" Maximus raised an inquiring eyebrow at his twin.

"Let me talk to her. You're scaring her."

"Hardly. She's been a thorn in my side since Vegas. My bet is she's The Chameleon we've been chasing."

"Let's discuss this later. We need to get out of here before the authorities are alerted." Alessandro, true to form, was trying to make peace. Like that was a possibility.

"Fine." Maximus went around and opened the driver's door. "She's your problem, bro." Why was he acting so oddly over the female and losing his legendary cool? Damned if he knew.

He gunned the engine of the BMW, keeping his concentration on driving and not on the female between them in the front seat. Trinity's every tiny movement seemed designed to pull his attention away from the roadway and back onto her. Her scent was filling him with thoughts that defied logic.

An hour later, he parked in the garage behind the deserted villa, wanting to be done with it and gain some perspective. The estate, situated in the middle of nowhere, was an hour out of Rome. The peace and quiet it afforded would give them time to think, something they both desperately needed to get their heads on straight.

"You can't keep me here. I have rights," Trinity protested as they made short work between them of hustling her up the path and into the villa. The house was sprawling and equipped with every modern marvel known to man, including a covered inner courtyard that included a pool. It would ensure a comfortable stay and also privacy, as no one stayed at the villa full-time. He'd just need to remember to call the day staff to cancel their duties until further notice. The last thing they needed was anyone knowing what was about to happen here.

"It's just until we get some things cleared up," Alessandro said.

Maximus gave a quick glance around, strode to the kitchen and picked out a length of rope from a drawer. He gave it a quick tug to check if it was strong enough, then advanced on his prey.

"You don't need to do this," Trinity protested, her eyes widening in concern.

"Right. And soon as we turn our backs, you'll be running from us. Tell me differently, *tesoro*."

She kept a close watch on him, her body rigid and unyielding. When he reached for her hands in preparation for tying her up, she struggled violently to pull away, making the sleeve of her blouse ride up. Angry teeth marks in a half circle were clearly visible in the overhead lighting.

"What's this?" Maximus barked. The thought of a wolf biting this tiny human made him ill beyond measure, though it explained the slight scent of animal they'd noticed earlier. A need for vengeance rose from deep inside, heating the marrow of his bones to such a degree that he vibrated with the intense emotion. The memory of what they had witnessed in Vegas when they were home for the wedding shot through him. All the air squeezed from his lungs as he relived it, the terrible pain and suffering of the human before she died. It left him raw. Angry.

"A dog bit me. A few weeks back, at a dive motel in Vegas, it came out of nowhere and attacked me." She rubbed at the wound. "It's slowly getting better."

"That's not a dog bite. It's from a Nomad," Alessandro said, coming forward and reaching to touch the wound.

They shared a look. *Damn it.* This was a game changer. They couldn't let her go now. The bloody dogs might be controlling her mind and she may not even know it.

"What's a Nomad?" Trinity asked, her brows knitting together.

"She could die from this, during the change. What are we going to do?" Alessandro asked him, obviously not wanting to state the facts aloud and scare their tiny hostage. Even hearing it in his mind was more than he could bear at that moment. She might be a handful, but she drew him on some elementary level that made him overly concerned for her welfare. The strong new urge building in him to protect her defied reason. Surely, he would feel the same way about any human in need? But down deep, he knew he was fooling himself. It was *this* human he wanted to protect.

"Use the clue to find the artifact," he answered, trying to keep the worry out of his tone and alerting Alessandro to the situation. He needn't have bothered. It was obvious his brother was just as concerned as him and wasn't troubling himself to hide it. At least, not from him. His twin's worry was spilling over into all his thoughts.

"What about Trinity?"

"We take her with us. Keep her safe." At least they could protect her from other wolves, if not from the changes going on in her body that no one had any control over. The primal urge to race out into the night and find the priceless chalice nearly overcame all his good sense. Just thinking of what had happened all those years ago when they'd been powerless to aid their friend sent him into near moon frenzy, a powerful state that left no room for reasoning or understanding. He'd been there

before and vowed never to return. He had to keep a tight grip on himself. It had never been more important than now.

"What are you *not* telling me?" Trinity asked, hands on hips. He hadn't had the heart to tie her up after discovering the damning evidence.

He shared another look with his brother. *"We can't tell her. At least not yet."*

"Nothing. It was just a surprise — the bite. Now, we need to know everything that happened in Vegas. And don't leave out one tiny detail," he said, warning her. He needed to get a handle on this thing. Now.

"I thought what happened in Vegas stayed there?" she said in a flippant manner.

He'd had enough. "We can't protect you if we don't know all the facts." For the first time he wished he could *mesmer* her like a vampire was capable of. *Make her spill the facts in record time.*

"Protect me from what?" She kept her glance locked on his. Her eyes were deep beautiful pools of wonder. The sparks jumping between them electrified the air. He glanced at her lips, desperately wanting to claim them. The scent of her arousal became stronger and the urge to crush her to him nearly overcame him. He leaned in closer and her lips opened. A tiny pink tongue lightly licked over them, enticing him.

It was all together too damn much.

He took hold of her. The lust in her eyes bore witness to her need. She wanted him, as much as he wanted her. When he pressed his lips to hers, touched them for the first time, the lust to claim her fired his blood. He didn't care that Alessandro stood right there, another presence in the room. For those first few seconds that he searched her mouth with his tongue, tasted her essence, he was all but alone with her, taken to a place he had never been before.

When she broke away to lay sweet kisses on his neck, his cock throbbed with need. "What do you think you're doing?" he asked.

"Just a gal who knows what she wants." Her tone had changed, had a new coyness, confusing him. Was she in heat? Or just trying to distract them into giving herself time to escape?

"*She might be coming into heat.*" Alessandro's voice bore into his thoughts. "*It might happen this quickly.*"

"*Maybe.*" But it felt like something more than that just plain lust. Something far more powerful. The connection between them was beyond amazing. Could Alessandro feel it as well? Too much was at stake here to make a mistake now. He couldn't afford to lower his guard. They needed to trust her, but it was too soon for that. She'd have to be tested first.

"*You kiss her, bro. See what you think.*" Was she the fabled one? Their Forever Mate?

Maximus reluctantly moved away, letting Alessandro come in closer to Trinity. If she was their destined mate, there could be no jealousy.

And no turning back.

Chapter Six

Alessandro

Trinity's pupils had darkened. Her normally innocent-appearing bluebell-colored eyes looked to be out of focus as well, with a smoldering lust dancing in their depths. Unable to stop himself, he ran a finger down her velvet cheek. "So soft," he murmured.

"Kiss me," she said, as bold as any superheroine.

He swept the thick silky hair back from her face with both hands, then bent his head down to hers. A fire erupted between as he pressed his lips to hers, gaining entrance to her warm mouth. Her breath enticed him, sweet with the scent of cherries. When she pressed herself against his lengthening cock, it was all he could do not to throw her onto the floor. Strip the clothes from her curvy body and kiss her all over. Fill her with his knot and his essence.

"You feel it too?"

"Yes. A thousand times yes."

A soft buzzing erupted and made Trinity pull away from him abruptly. She slipped the phone from her pocket, glanced at the text then went to shove it back inside her pants.

Maximus made a grab for it and took it away before she could react. Her expression turned to one of anger.

Have you got it? the text read.

He showed his twin the damning evidence. The message was clear, sent from the House of Ribelle's enforcer, Rocco. They both instantly knew what that meant. The female had betrayed them.

Maximus grabbed the phone and threw it on the floor, breaking it to smithereens.

"What are you doing?" Trinity shouted.

"Those bastards can track us on that device. You've been in touch with our sworn enemies. The Ribelle curs," Maximus near shouted, his anger apparent in his smoldering complexion and flashing brown eyes.

"I don't have a clue what you're talking about." But her words sounded less than forthright.

"What part of 'sworn enemies' don't you get?"

"This is not the way, bro," Alessandro said calmly, interrupting the stalemate. "Trinity, I'm not certain if you understand the depth of our antagonism with the Ribelles. For centuries, our families have been at war."

She remained silent, her expression tight. But at least she was listening. *How much to tell her and not cause even more trouble?*

"This bad blood that exists between the houses, it can cause unforeseen tragic outcomes for either side. People have died due to it." He cleared his throat, thinking of his sister, the pain that had never gone entirely filling him once more. "We're just worried about you. We want to keep you safe. And getting between the houses of Luceres and Ribelle—that's dangerous. You have to pick a side and be loyal. Soon."

"Why are you giving her a choice?"

"Because it's the right thing to do."

"What if I choose the Ribelle? Will you let me go?"

Alessandro rubbed his aching head as Maximus growled. What did she need to hear?

"The two houses are not equal. We do things differently. The Ribelle…well, suffice to say they're not into women's liberation. They want to dominate their women—"

"And you don't? Not what I'm seeing here."

"We won't make you do anything you don't want or ask us to do. We don't mind-control others like the Ribelle are all-too-well known to do."

"No one controls my mind! That's crazy." She looked horrified at the very idea.

"Do you normally choose to go after artifacts so far from Rome and one that you seem to know little about? Was that all your doing?"

"Maybe." She rubbed her forehead, looking confused. "It pays well and I need money."

Now they were getting to the crux of the matter. "We'll give you all the money you need without endangering your safety. No questions asked."

"Really? You'd give me money for no reason other than I asked?" She looked nonplused, obviously not seeing that coming.

"What do you need? Name a figure."

"I prefer to work for the money. I'm not a charity case." She shook her head, her beautiful blonde-streaked brown hair spilling out around her shoulders and curling at her tiny waist. It was all he could do not to ravish her on the spot. *Such a difficult female. Such an incredible female.*

"Work for us and we'll pay you twice what the Ribelle were offering," Maximus jumped in.

"Good thinking, bro."

"Okay, I can help you with finding the artifact and you can pay me for that. But be aware, they offered me a really good price. And I'll have to contact them to cancel the contract."

"Great. It's a deal then. We're off to the wilds of Alaska tomorrow at the crack of dawn."

"You didn't ask me for the sum? And I insist on a benefits package that includes air travel and hotel costs."

The twins shared a grin. *"Does she have any idea how rich we are?"*

"No problem. We would have insisted on paying your way, no matter what."

"And I need a new phone."

"Anything else?"

"I need to call my family. Let them know what the deal is." A haunted expression crossed her face and Alessandro had to wonder why? *Family problems?*

"Of course. You can use my phone." He dug out his cell phone and handed it to her.

"And I need some privacy," she said, raising her eyebrows.

"Take any room you want." Alessandro waved his hand around. "Consider our home yours."

"This place belongs to you?"

"Yes, just one of many," Alessandro said with a smile. *"She really has no idea. This is going to be fun."*

"Maybe. But we'll keep close tabs on her anyway. Until we're certain."

Chapter Seven

Trinity

Trinity sent a text terminating her contact with the Ribelles, then punched in her parents' home phone number. She sat on a bed in one of the guestrooms, trying to push away the discomfort of being in a strange place with such hot, virile men. *Yeah, and rich to boot.* Of course, that brought on a flash of heat she didn't need right at the moment when she was about to talk to her mom.

She rubbed her thighs together, wishing she could supress the ridiculous lust she felt around the Luceres twins. It was beyond bothersome. What was she thinking? Now she was tied into seeing them twenty-four-seven until the artifact was found. She truly did need her head examined. Much like her parents did, for marrying three days after they'd first met in Vegas. Something she was *never* going to do, tie herself through marriage to a man. On the other hand, the quickie nuptials had lasted thirty-plus years. But another part of her couldn't wait to see what developed with the two alpha males. *I mean, they're just so incredibly hot.*

"Hi, Mom, it's Trinity."

"Sweetheart! Are you okay? We wondered when we didn't hear from you." Her mom sounded worried, and she instantly felt guilty over not checking in earlier.

"I'm fine. Just got caught up in making a deal for going after another artifact."

"I hope you asked for more than last time. We need more help, Trinity, your dad's ailing again and unable to work. You're out biggest hope, girl."

She could just imagine what her dad was 'ailing' from. The bottom of a bottle was the usual culprit. At least her contributions might one day buy him help that would really work. Rehab often took more than one go. She just needed to make the money to provide the best care for him to kick his addiction. What was it Frost had said so succinctly that had finally helped her to better understood the powerful draw? *Drugs take you to hell, disguised as heaven.*

"Yes, they pay well and all expenses included. I was calling to let you know that I'm leaving the country again for Alaska. I might be out of cell range for a few days and I didn't want you to worry." She rubbed her eyes, feeling antsy and not like herself of a sudden. She swore she could hear whispers of unseen beings in the air. What was that about?

"Alaska! What on earth kind of treasure are you going way up there for? Nothing but Eskimos and those back-to-the-landers." Her mother sounded outraged. It was not her intention to cause her worry, just reassure her about money.

"They aren't called Eskimos anymore, Mom. I think the right word is Inuit. And someone hid the item near Barrow centuries ago — worth a fortune. But I gotta go. I'll wire the money into your account before I leave. Okay?" She hated to ask the Luceres for the money upfront, but what choice did she have?

"Good. Thank you, Trinity. I wish your sisters could provide like you do," her mother said with a sigh.

"They will when they can." It was left unsaid between them how much that would depend on her various family members deciding to work at fulltime jobs or use some of their God-given talents. So far, other than her own ability to count cards, nothing had shown up. They'd told her often enough that she was the lucky one who should accept the honor of doing the family's financial business as fair trade for the ability. Maybe they were right? She couldn't see her family go without, no matter what they needed. They had always been there for her.

She hung up and got to her feet to return the cell phone to its rightful owner and ask for an advance.

When she exited the room and reached the end of the hallway, she heard the brothers speaking and stopped to listen.

"The next full moon is on the twenty-first. Just a few days away. Not much margin for error. And you saw how she was acting, right?"

Though the twins were identical, she could hear the difference. It had to be Maximus talking with that more aggressive tone. Alessandro was the peacemaker, his brother the one she had to most look out for. *Volatile and dangerous.* They were both over-the-top-hot so no difference there.

"She will be reduced to instinct soon. We need to help her through it, see that she gets everything she needs."

What are they even talking about? Instincts and full moons?

"I got everything she needs right here." That was Maximus, and she could almost see him making an aggressive grab for his considerable package. *Oh yeah, beyond hot.*

"There's more to having a Forever Mate than sex. There's providing for her every need, seeing she stays in prime physical condition and is happy and contented to be with us. Keep her satisfied on every level and keep her safe."

A Forever Mate? What did that mean? The information dump had her head spinning and not in a good way.

"We'll play to our strengths. You keep her emotionally satisfied and I'll see to her baser needs. Works for me."

"That's not how this works and you know it. Damn it, Maximus! It's share and share alike. No room for petty jealousy and staking a separate claim."

She'd had enough. "What are you guys talking about? I'm nobody's plaything." She came out of hiding and confronted them.

"How much did you hear?" Maximus asked, his eyes narrowing.

"Enough to know that you're both not making a whole lot of sense. What does the full moon have to do with me? And what is a Forever Mate?"

"Come, sit, we'll talk. Can I offer you a cocktail before we eat?" Alessandro asked, his expression conciliatory and concerned.

"Sure. I definitely need a drink." *Or ten.*

"Great. We have a fully stocked bar, so what's your preference?"

"White wine's fine. Not too dry."

She perched on a highbacked stool at the island the pair were already sitting at. Alessandro held out a glass of Riesling to her and she took it, swallowing a few gulps to steady herself.

"It's good," she said. "Okay, spill."

The two brothers exchanged a look, then Alessandro nodded. She could see how close they were at that moment. Like they could communicate in ways that most people couldn't. Probably because they were twins. *Double the trouble,* came to mind. Or maybe it would be *double the fun*?

"You are going to undergo some changes that, scientifically speaking, will stretch your imagination to the limit."

"What kind of changes?"

"New cravings, new abilities—rather big changes. How have you been feeling of late? Since you were bitten?"

She took another large gulp of the wine and Maximus refilled her glass. She nodded her thanks. "I've been feeling a bit odd, okay?"

"In what ways?" Alessandro pressed.

"More confused than anything. Like, I'm not exactly sure that it was entirely my idea to go after the chalice, okay?" She was very uncomfortable admitting it. She was a woman who valued being in control of things. "I actually prefer gambling to artifact gathering. Cash is easier to acquire than having to fence an item. But I do have a buyer—or I did, until you guys came along."

Maximus growled. She gave him a startled glance, but when he didn't move or say anything else, she calmed down a bit.

"And just so you know, I've texted to cancel the contract."

"Were you able to reassure your parents?" Alessandro asked, making the conversation veer sideways. *Fine.* This she needed to get out on the table anyway.

"About that. I was wondering about a cash advance? My mother needs—"

"Of course. How do you want us to take care of that? Wire the funds to an account?" Alessandro asked.

"Yes, that would work. Do you have some paper and a pen? I'll write down the particulars for you. Umm, how much money are we talking about?"

"What do you need?" Alessandro asked.

She snorted. "Don't ask anyone in my family that question. There's no end to what they need."

"Does a million sound okay? For now?" Maximus asked.

She stared at the pair, half in shock. "Are you guys for real? That's a lot of money. Twenty times what the Ribelles offered me."

"No worries." Maximus handed her a pad of paper and a pencil.

She quickly wrote down all the facts from memory. *Not hard.* She'd done it so often before. She handed it back to Maximus.

"I'll take care of it straight away."

"Thank you."

"My pleasure, *tesoro*."

When Maximus left the room, she gave his twin a steady look. She felt he was her best bet for information.

"Okay, I want to know more about what's going on. And I want to know *now*."

Alessandro gave her a pensive look, running his fingers around the rim of his glass. *Such fine fingers too.* Well formed, sensitive, and yet with the look of being able to handle anything. She tore her mind away from admiring him for a moment to listen to his words carefully. "That bite you endured. It has consequences, as I told you. In five days, on the night of the full moon, your body will try to change you into a new form."

The light dawned. "You're kidding me, right? You're trying to tell me I'll shift to a werewolf, right? There's no such thing." How could the intelligent Luceres brothers believe in such things? They were highly respected scholars. It made no sense. Maybe *civilization is like a thin layer of ice upon a deep ocean of chaos and darkness*, like Werner Herzog suggested?

"I know, it's a lot to take in. But there is a history to this you are not aware of. Let me explain. This all began in Roman days during the founding of their capital."

He was taking it seriously. She frowned, an unsettled feeling knotting her stomach. *Too much wine and not enough to eat.*

"You're hungry. I'll get you some food before I explain." Alessandro got up and strode to the refrigerator and took out a platter of food, setting it on the island in front of her.

"Eat something. You'll feel better." His expression of genuine concern for her wellbeing made her pause. No one had cared to make sure she was comfortable in the past. It seemed everyone she met had an agenda, wanting something from her first as a kind of quid pro quo. It was nice to be thought of in this way. *Don't get too used to it, Trinity. When the job is over, we all go our separate ways. That's the way it's always been.*

She consumed a few tablespoons of the caviar in short order with the crisp, thin crackers supplied. The plump olives stuffed with red pepper were divine.

"Good," she said between mouthfuls. "Really good." She waved a hand at him. "I can listen while I eat. Go ahead. Continue."

"Okay. You are aware of the myth of Romulus and Remus and the founding of Rome? And the first she-wolf?"

She nodded, grabbing a pear. When she bit into it, juice burst over her tongue, offering the heavenly taste of perfectly ripened fruit. She swiped at a bit of juice that had run down her chin. "The nursing of the twins to keep them alive, then the argument over which of the seven hills to build upon."

"Right. While at that time in history, the House of Luceres and House of Ribelle were created. Later, there was another split and the final house was born—House of Anche. Centuries later, we all have casinos in Vegas, though our family has expanded worldwide."

"That's some family history." Her mind boggled at being able to connect an ancestry back so far in time. "But you can't possibly think that all those people are werewolves, right? That's crazy. Oops, sorry, I don't mean that *you're* crazy, per se, but the idea, *wow*, it's out there." She was mellow now from the food and drink. Actually, she figured that Alessandro was more than likely just pulling her leg. *Trying for a reaction.* What was his angle?

But now that one need was fully satiated, another reared up. *Lust.* It filled her with amazing speed, making every nerve tingle with excitement in her body.

She glanced at the fine specimen of manhood sitting enticingly close, his fragrance of clean musk and spicy cinnamon filling her with anticipation. They were alone. No obligations tonight. Her family was well taken care of. Surely, she could have something for herself now? A memory of memories to keep close during the long barren nights to come. She'd had lots of lonely times. Far too many to count, actually.

"So, when is the camera crew going to pop out?"

He frowned at her, his quizzical boyish expression charming her further.

"You know, to tell me I've been had?" She waved her hands around.

"No, you're not hearing me. You will turn into a werewolf at the next full moon or—" He stopped himself, his expression dire.

"Or what?"

"Nothing. We will find the Lupus Sanguis Chalice and make things right."

"I can think of something else that just might save me," she teased, leaning over and running a forefinger over his plush bottom lip, hardly believing her own audacity. The wine had her feeling like she was on fire, her body not quite her own, but ready to enjoy everything that being young and healthy allowed. And then some.

"Much as I want you right here and now-- make no mistake of that—I want to save you from yourself even more. You don't realize that with such a powerful aphrodisiac as werewolf DNA racing through your bloodstream, you're not as quite in control as you normally would be. I can't take advantage of you knowing that."

It took her a few seconds to realize he was shutting her down. She blinked, her thoughts in disarray. *Well, hell.*

"Not sure Maximus would feel the same," she fired back, more in reflex than in giving her words proper consideration.

"My brother and I are united in wanting to help you." Though he kept his verbal message strong, she could see just a slight hesitation on his part when a split second of worry flashed in his dreamy brown eyes. Oh yeah, Maximus could easily be corrupted. But it would be so much more fun to get Alessandro to take her up on the invitation. Well, she had days ahead to tease them both. The trip was looking more and more inviting by the second.

What am I thinking? There was no way she'd come between brothers. Family was family. What the hell, maybe she'd just do them both. The normally totally out-of-bounds idea came out of the blue, shocking her to the very core of her being. Oh, but it was so wanton and exhilarating. What *was* going on with her? Maybe there was something to this idea of being infected by a bite. If lust was one of the awesome symptoms.

Maximus strode back into the room, a satisfied expression on his handsome mug. "All taken care of."

A *ding* on her phone heralded an incoming text. She picked it up and clicked on it.

Money has arrived. Enjoy Alaska and don't forget to buy presents for your sisters.

What kind of presents could she buy in Alaska that her sisters wouldn't scoff at? All of them were so darn fussy. Not to mention she was supposed to be working too. Someone had to earn that million dollars. God, what was she thinking? Accepting a million dollars for something that might turn into a wild-goose chase?

Well, it wasn't like Maximus and Alessandro couldn't afford it. But still, it didn't sit right. When the day came and she could make all her own decisions, things would be different. No more doing things that rode on the cusp of ethics. Instead, she'd live her life totally on the up and up. *Give to charities and feel good about myself.* That would be a *thousand* times better.

"My family says thanks." They'd said no such thing, but she didn't want the brothers to think poorly of them and their stinginess about their incredible generosity.

The brothers nodded nonchalantly, like paying a million dollars for a week's work was an everyday occurrence.

"Don't worry, we intend to get our money's worth on this trip," Maximus said with a slight leer. Oh yeah, he could be easily led astray.

"I know I'm more than up for an adventure…artifact or anything else rare that crosses my path," she shot back. Then sat stunned and yet pleased at her newfound confidence. Yup, this was looking to be a fine, fine trip all right.

Chapter Eight

Maximus

Oh, but the little *tesoro* blatantly suggesting she was up for a good time was a hot one. And she cared about her family to boot — good characteristics to find in one human being. He was certain now she only counted cards in their casinos to see her family looked after. He admired that a great deal. Their pack aided fellow members in all ways possible. Trinity would fit right in.

Then a harsh worry sluiced through him. She might not be around for long, if her change didn't go well. Fear struck him, hard. Already he had begun to care for her, try as he might to keep it to himself. If he began to enjoy having her around too much and she was lost to them at the next full moon, he wasn't sure if he could handle the grief that consumed any wolf that lost their Forever Mate. It was best to not get in over his head now. *Pull back and enjoy her company, but don't cross that line.* But a part of him knew it was going to be tough. She drew him on every level.

"Say, how about we do some shots? Toast our week in the land of the midnight sun," Trinity suggested, her expression fueled by mischief. She gave off a rich musky, feminine fragrance that stirred his blood…and hardened his cock.

The werewolf serum was affecting her, more than she realized. Keeping control of his own lust was probably going to be of the difficult things he would be called upon to do around the tantalizing woman.

"She came onto me as well, bro. I explained what's going on, but I don't think she believed me."

"She'd do us both, bro."

"That doesn't make it right."

But Trinity didn't intend to make it easy. She jumped up, grabbing a bottle of tequila from the bar and three shot glasses, poured them full of the golden liquor and handed him and Alessandro one each. She picked up the third one for herself.

"Bottoms up!" she said, a wicked smile adorning her beautiful face. As soon as they'd downed the first, she poured another.

"What's the toast to this time?" Alessandro asked, deliberately recapping the tall bottle of liquor.

Trinity pouted at his actions, then held the shot glass high in the air. "To a trip packed with all the fun one can imagine." She drank it down, licking the final drops from the rim of the glass, pretending to ignore than both, having to know they were watching her every movement.

"We have to have one more. It's unlucky not to have three drinks and we need to toast what we're going after." And before either of them could react, she'd uncapped the bottle and refilled the glasses.

"Okay, last one," Alessandro said with a clear warning in his tone.

"To finding the Lupus Sanguis Chalice," Maximus said. *And to saving your life, tesoro.*

"To the chalice," she said, swallowing down the alcohol in short order. Her eyes sparked with intent. The fragrance of her lust intensified and Maximus had all he could manage not to grab her right then and there and kiss those soft pink lips once more. To pull that curvy little body up tight to his, devour every inch of her. Make her know the true meaning of lust and desire and power. Drive her crazy with his tongue before thrusting into her so many times with his hard cock she lost all sense of everything else.

"And now it's time for bed," Alessandro said, taking the bottle from Trinity who had managed to grab hold of it again.

"Great—which bedroom is ours?"

Dead silence greeted her question. Oh, but he wanted to take her up on that sassy challenge. But one glance at his thunderstruck brother and he decided against it. There would be plenty of time on the trip for fun and games. Way up north, the three of them alone bundled into a hunting lodge or hotel... It was sounding better and better.

"We have to be up early in the morning, so it's off to bed. Alone. And lock your door, Trinity. I don't want anyone sleepwalking tonight."

"Yes, Daddy," Trinity said, swaying a bit as she got up off her chair.

Maximus rushed to her side, getting there at the same exact moment as his twin. They escorted their guest down the hall to a guest room.

"Thank you, guys. You've been just peachy." Trinity gave them a small queenly wave of her slender fingers as they let both reluctantly let go of her.

"You going to be okay?" Alessandro asked.

"Great. Hate to sleep alone. But I'll manage." She closed the door on both of them. Maximus could hear giggles erupting behind the flimsy barrier.

"She doesn't intend to make it easy."

"No, let's have a nightcap," Maximus suggested. Alcohol left their systems fairly quickly—no matter how much they drank, they never got drunk, just pleasantly relaxed. *And horny if there's a willing female anywhere in the vicinity.*

"Yeah, why not."

They headed back down the hallway.

"So we're agreed we don't touch her until this is all over?"

Maximus snorted with derision as Alessandro splashed brandy into two glasses. "She's not in a true heat—not yet. If she were, she'd be all over us, not teasing us. That's permission, bro, if you don't understand mating cues."

"I don't have to tell you the risks of doing that, right?"

They both took a long drink of the soothing liquor, contemplating the stark facts.

"Way to make a man lose his hard-on."

"Well, I'm off to bed." Alessandro finished his drink and got up. "I'd suggest you do the same. We leave early in the morning."

"Soon."

He watched his brother stride off, his mind focusing on other things. Well, one thing — the female lying in bed not thirty feet away from where he sat and stewed was horny as hell. Her siren call made his cock twitch and lengthen. She was going to be theirs, one way or the other. He couldn't think of after, of what might happen, not now. He wanted to live *this* moment, filled with anticipation that had his head spinning, feeling the urge to allow himself the freedom of being right out of control. The night air swirled around him, alive with a pulsing energy that fired his flesh into a taunt alertness, making him ready to spring into action at any second.

A splash woke him from his musings. What was this? Someone in the pool? An interloper? He was out of his seat and entering the covered inner courtyard in a blur of movement.

Small waves on the surface of the water surrounded their guest as she bobbed up and down, one second exposing her beautiful, full, naked breasts, the next up to her shoulders in the heated water of the pool. She waved at him, a wide smile lighting up her face.

"Come on in. I don't bite."

Fuck. Of all the words to use, she had to send him a reminder of the precariousness of her position. But then, if there was such a little bit of time left, surely it made sense to enjoy every single second of it? Life turned on such momentous occasions. *Once lost, never regained. Even civilizations have come tumbling down in mere minutes.*

Port Royal vanishing in an earthquake and Pompeii under volcanic ashes came to mind, along with so many other catastrophes he didn't want to take time to consider with a willing female right before him in the here and now. *Time to put the scholar away and live for the man and wolf.*

He began to unbuckle his belt then quickly removed his clothing, dropping them poolside. This was not an opportunity to turn down. She wasn't in true lust yet. She had to know what she was up to. What man in his right mind could ignore such an amazing woman ascending to her peak of power and beauty?

"I'm liking what I'm seeing," she teased, splashing water his way as he dropped into the pool. Using his powerful arms to cross the distance between them, he was confronting her in a matter of seconds, looming over her. They both trod water, weightless.

"No more than I do. You are beautiful. Beautiful beyond compare." He reached for her, drawing her in tight against him. She came willingly, snuggling in so close his breath released from his body in a wild whoosh.

He grabbed the back of her head, crushing her lips with his, their breath mingling. Everything else blurred into oblivion as he took her, twining his tongue with hers and tasting the sweetness within. He kissed her and he became a man possessed, hungry, and needy, unable to get enough.

Moving his hand to grasp one of her firm young breasts, he brushed the tightened nipple with a thumb before using his lips to suck it into his mouth, tugging on her without mercy. She squealed with delight. He danced his tongue over the firm flesh, giving full attention to one perfect orb, then the other. His head just below the waterline, she arched her body to give him better access.

They locked glances when he broke the surface of the pool for a breath of air, shaking his head to remove the water drops that dripped down his face. Lust darkened her pupils, reflected back from his own.

Without taking his eyes off hers, he grasped her legs and pulled them up to circle around his waist, giving him complete access. He slid up against her, pushing his hardened cock into the soft folds, searching for her channel. She arched her back further, spreading herself for him.

"Do it *now*. I need you inside me."

No going back. The urgency of her words pushed him over the edge.

He drove him cock into her with enough force to seat himself fully in one mighty thrust. Her channel enclosed him like the finest velvet, tighter than the perfect glove and hotter than he could have imagined. She was ready, needy, so prepared for him she pushed herself even tighter against his groin, giving him complete permission to fuck her as he saw fit.

"Yes, take it all, my beautiful *tesoro*. Let me inside, open for me. Keep nothing back. I want all of you. Give it to me."

She obliged his every demand, responding to his every nuance, her hot little body taking all he had to give. He crushed her to him, his flesh feeling on fire, his cock harder than it had ever been. And yet it demanded more. His knot pulsed. It began to grow and tighten inside her channel, filling her further, tightening almost beyond imagining. Instead of pulling back, she appeared to relish it, screaming her pleasure aloud. He thumbed her clit, circling it and tugging on it to keep her fully aroused. His knot would push her over the edge. Could she handle all of him? Never had he wanted so badly to fully knot with a female.

"Yes! Fuck me harder. Harder!" Her eyes grow rounder and larger. A depth of emotion he'd never seen in another female's expression kept him mesmerized, yet gave him pause. Was this how it felt? When the female was destined to be their Forever Mate?

He let his cock lead the way now, doing what it had to do. *What it was born for.* Lock into her pussy, destroy any barrier in his way and make her want only him. Bite and claim her for all time.

His knot demanded and she took it all as they rode the experience out in long, satisfying moments together. Their bodies one, their flesh consumed by passion. She mewled, her eyes rolling backward and exposing the whites, her lips twitching. His sac drew up tight and his essence surged outward, filling her with his seed. He growled with the sensation, then lowered his head to mark her, his teeth grazing her collarbone. Suddenly, a howl came in the distance. It made him pause. *Who was that?* Yanking his head away, he heard the call, screaming bloody murder at him to stop.

Instead of biting her, he withdrew his fangs and drew her closer. For many long, beautiful minutes they climaxed, shudders and tremors of intense pleasure coursing back and forth between them. When the sensations finally subsided, he waited for her to speak.

"I had no idea, no idea at all it could be like that," she said in a trembling voice. "Is it always like this?"

"Yes." Then what he had just done, the complications of his actions, swept over him in a wave of dark emotion. *What if something happens to her now?* He shuddered and crushed her to him, his worry overcoming everything else. *What have I done?* He would be destroyed now, if anything bad affected this tiny human.

"Hey, you're squeezing the life out of me!" she protested, pushing back at him.

He picked her up in his arms and swam with her to the water's edge, boosting her out. How such a small body could hold such an incredible human being boggled his mind. She was made for him, born to be with him, as scary as it sounded. Would it be the same for his brother? The odds were in favor of that being the case. She and Alessandro had already shared a kiss, and no doubt more would be forthcoming. *Oh fuck.* Could Alessandro live through the pain of losing her, if it came to that? No, neither of them could bite her, claim her, knowing that. That was why his brother had stopped him. Had kept him from making such a terrible mistake…one he couldn't ever come back from.

Consumed by guilt, he nabbed a towel for himself, wrapping it around his waist before grabbing another one. He began drying her off, trying his best to hide his seething emotions that were so unlike him. Years spent in the hallowed halls of learning had dampened down his wilder instinct, at least until now. Perhaps that was the problem. Though when they'd been home for the wedding, when he and his twin had been accosted by his plenitude of cousins after the ceremony, they had all run pack wild that night. They'd needed the distraction after looking in on the female who was dying due to the change going deadly for her. The terrifying image cut front and center of his mind, making him sick to his stomach. Apparently, he wasn't very good at hiding his feelings when it came to this, because she laid a gentle hand on his cheek, cupping his jaw.

"What's wrong, Maximus? Have I done something to upset you?" Her blue eyes, still softened with huge pupils from the passion they'd shared, flashed with a look of pain that tugged at his heartstrings.

"No. Of course not."

He hadn't meant to sound so stern. But his brain refused to let go of the fearful nature of the change when it involved a vulnerable human.

"What's going on in here?" Alessandro asked, striding up to them, all sweaty from running back to the Villa, his expression one of outrage. "What did you do, Maximus? My God, did you hurt her?"

Chapter Nine

Trinity

Trinity glanced from one twin to the other, shaky from still being in the throes of an intense passion she'd never known existed. The experience had rocked her world *and* her view of herself. Now, she had no idea how to act. Lust had overcome her better judgment, something that had *never* happened before. Guilt struck hard. Had she just come between the brothers, something she would never do deliberately?

She'd been totally incapable of stopping herself, but was that even an excuse? But deep down inside, she knew she'd do it again, with either of them, if the opportunity presented itself. She just needed to grow a pair. *Keep myself strong. Not be swayed by delicious fragrances, bad-boy glances and tight pecs.*

"No, she's not hurt," Maximus said. His expression downright stony, he wasn't giving anything away. And yet not five minutes ago, he'd been the best damn lover imaginable, making her feel so unbelievably happy to be alive. Hell, she was still discombobulated, tingling in all manner of exquisite ways.

"I'm right here and I can speak for myself," she said, unable to keep the upset out of her tone. The dynamics had just gotten weird. She'd learned a long time ago that there was a second or two when her instincts would kick in, letting her know that things were shifting when she was putting herself at risk when gambling, and it was a warning to pay attention to. It had kept her safe in the past. *Time to get the hell away from this situation.*

"Are you okay?" Alessandro asked, his normally calm expression shut down by worry.

"I'm fine. And if you'll excuse me, I'm going to bed."

Tucking the towel over her breasts, she turned to make her exit.

"Hold on, Trinity," Alessandro said, coming closer to confront her. She refused to look him in the eye, knowing her weakness for the Luceres twins all too well now.

"I'm just peachy, thank you very much." Okay, that came out a bit sarcastic.

"No, you're not. What do you need? Just ask." His high body heat and delectable scent was almost her undoing. She had an intense urge to throw herself at him that she overcame with extreme willpower. This couldn't happen again. *Where in the hell did my normally ordered mind go? This all started in Vegas when that damn dog bit me, like something grabbed hold and won't let go.*

"I need to go to bed, lock my door and pretend this didn't happen. Okay with you?" Now she had slipped into bitch territory, making her doubt herself even more. She rubbed her forehead. Maybe she was coming down with something? She was feeling light-headed and dizzy. What was she doing here anyway? With two men born with silver spoons in their mouths? The words of her mother worked through her mind, making her even more lacking in confidence. *"Take money from the rich, but keep that tender heart protected, Trinity, men born to wealth only want one thing from a beautiful girl and it's not her cooking skills. Trust me."*

Suddenly she was swept up by a strong pair of arms. *Not helping.* All she wanted was to bed *this* Luceres now. *What the fuck?*

"What are you doing?" she demanded, trying her best not to show where her mind was at.

"Carrying you to bed. You're done in, thanks to my brother." *Well, not exactly.* But she felt the bristling nature that had erupted between the pair again. *Yeah, partly my fault.* The thought put a damper on her lust for the moment.

Within seconds, Alessandro had her back in her bedroom. He pulled a nightgown over her head like she was a child before tucking her into the cool, ridiculously high-thread-count sheets. She settled back and watched him from under heavy-lidded eyes. Being looked after didn't suck one bit.

"Thank you," she said, so close to dreamland that her body had finally relaxed, all the adrenaline of the sex act draining away.

"For what?"

"For being so nice to me."

He hesitated, as if he wanted to say something important, then thought better of it, turning off the light and murmuring, "Sleep well, little one. We'll talk more in the morning."

Lying there alone in the dark, she vowed to keep her emotions locked up. *Yes, Mom, they do want just one thing from me. But I want it to. And when this week is ended, it's back to the real world for me. No regrets.* She knew where she belonged, and it was not in the high society of billionaires. She was just plain Trinity, a girl who had always worked hard to keep the wolf from the door. They'd never look twice at her anyway if she couldn't help them with their quest and wasn't the only female in their vicinity at the moment.

The last thing she heard before she drifted off to sleep was the pair having a heated argument.

Chapter Ten

Alessandro

"What the fuck was all that about?" He confronted his twin, standing so close that Maximus had to deal with him or lose face.

"Well, you've met her, right? How in the hell was I supposed to turn that down? She was skinny-dipping in the pool, her breasts like marble in the moonlight, the nipples peaked and perfect. Ripe for the taking, bro."

"You a damn poet now? You know what's at stake, yet you still do this? What the hell were you thinking, Maximus?"

"I wasn't, okay? I was in the throes of a wild passion I didn't see coming. You'd have done the same. Try to tell me differently. At least she smells better now with my scent on her instead of that Nomad's."

Alessandro raked his hands through his hair, his body ready to undergo the change. He tamped the feeling down. No good would come of them fighting.

He'd gone for a midnight run to clear his head, and he'd come back to *this*. His brother doing exactly the wrong thing. Putting himself at risk. His heart most of all, damn it.

"Fuck, man, we've got to get ourselves together. You think I don't want to do what you did? You got to pull on the shield. Put on all your resources into it and use that passion to find the chalice. That's the only hope left for us. You know that, right?"

"I know. It won't happen again. We're united on this quest, bro, I promise you that. We will find the chalice and save our kind. It's what we were born to do."

They shared a tight embrace, their dread of what was coming if they didn't find the artifact that would save Trinity's life their only focus.

"Okay, sleep now, bro."

They stalked off to their separate rooms. Alessandro threw himself on top of the bed, still dressed in the jeans and tee he'd scrambled into before confronting his brother. Though furious at his twin's behavior, he understood it on a deeper level all too well. Trinity's pull was no less than the magnetic pull of True North, impossible to ignore. Though Alessandro was certain he wouldn't be sleeping tonight with all the tension seething inside the villa, he fell into a restless slumber before dawn, the luminal world drawing him in.

The dream came on suddenly, freezing the marrow in his bones.

A cairn built of field stone in the shape of a stylized human appeared in shadow through the hazy, freezing mist that lashed with a driving force at his exposed skin. Against a backdrop of pure white, the squat feature loomed, calling to him on a deeper subconscious level. It beckoned to him, as if it would speak, before vanishing in a matter of seconds. An avalanche screaming down the mountainside had overcome it, burying it under tons of snow. Too late. The words came unbidden into his mind, making his pulse race with raw fear. Too late for what? Tell me!

He woke up with a startle, the buried man of ice and stone foremost in his mind. Why had he dreamed of an inukshuk? A poignant feature handed down from the Scots to the Inuit to establish landmarks on endless terrain. Was it a foreboding premonition, having it vanish under the snow? What were they going to be too late for? *No. It can't be that.* He jumped from the bed. The clockface on the nightstand read five o'clock, too early to leave. *Fuck it.* He'd shower and be ready before the others got up.

Striding into the kitchen a few minutes later, hair still damp and mind still pre-occupied with the ramifications of the dream, he went first to the huge sleek refrigerator and grabbed a selection of items. Bacon, sausage, eggs, cheese, butter, croissants and jam should fuel up everyone's body for what would most likely become an arduous trip through the frozen tundra of Alaska's northernmost tip. Werewolves and anyone in the process of change needed constant food and water to stay in their peak condition.

The change.

Though the words sounded innocuous, the result could be devastating. The memory of being back in Vegas for the wedding and seeing the young female so ill and in such terrible pain ate at his soul. *No.* He shook his head. He wouldn't go there. He'd vow instead to help Trinity through it, help Maximus through it. Because even though his brother had done the wrong thing last night, now, he was in worse peril. And Alessandro had to step up to protect him, at all costs.

Shoving all such dire thoughts aside, he made the calls to make arrangements to get them to Alaska then got down to work in the kitchen. Soon the fragrant scents of bacon and sausage frying in separate pans filled the kitchen with a sense of home. Large brunches were his families' speciality, especially on Sundays. He'd missed the interactions since he and his twin had been away so much these past years, scouring the earth for the chalice. The friendly interactions over food and drink lasted for hours, everyone catching up with one another. A family of mostly males could be boisterous, and his was no different.

How his mother had put up with being the only female defied comprehension. But she'd handled it with style and grace, always the provider of comfort and food. And now she had Everly as her daughter-in-law. One she-wolf on her side. The thought of him and Maximus never having that with Trinity, of being unable to bring her home to meet his family, made his throat ache with unshed tears, slamming into him with a terrible force, about to drive him to his knees with the pain. *Fuck, stay strong. This, too, shall pass.*

"Whatever you're cooking smells damn good, bro," Maximus said, joining him and clapping him on the back. "Anything I can do?"

"Check on Trinity and let her know breakfast is nearly ready." He studiously ignored his roiling thoughts and pulled the bacon from the pan, draining it on paper towels before adding the eggs to fry in the hot oil. Time was too precious now for anything but forging ahead and solving the dire circumstances they found themselves in.

"Sure." When his brother strode away, he buttered the freshly toasted bread and began to plate the food. *Just keep busy. Stay focused.*

The table now covered with a huge feast, he stood back with satisfaction. Maximus and Trinity came into the room and his breath squeezed at seeing her again. She looked so beautiful with her skin scrubbed and her hair freshly washed and hanging down her back. She smiled at him rather shyly and sat where he indicated. Her coyness of the night before had all but disappeared. *Halleluiah for that small favor.* But a big part of him wished he'd been in his brother's place. Been chosen. Now they had to keep the course, stay hands-off until this was all resolved. *Not going to be easy, not by a long shot.* His cock was already thickening just being near her, breathing in that lovely scent that defied description. He wanted nothing more than to be consumed by his passion for her.

He cleared his throat and instructed, "Eat all you can. We have a big journey ahead of us."

All three of them dived into the food, draining the platters in far less time than it had taken to cook. When everyone had had their fill, he pulled the slip of paper from his pocket and reread the passage.

"Those that seek the mother's blessing of blood and bone,

Shall find it hidden far from here in coldest depths of ice and stone.

In newer worlds, the tracks appear,

Upon a land of midnight sun,

The highest point of land is near, and shall reveal when all is clear."

"Must be Barrow, Alaska—that's the highest point in the land of the midnight sun. Oh, just a second, the name was changed a few years back. It's now called Utqiaġvik," Maximus said.

"Yes, I agree. Okay, let's grab whatever you need. I've had the Lear jet fueled and it should be delivered any moment. The flight plan has been filed. We'll in Alaska by late today. Any questions?"

"That's the right location. I have no doubt of it," Trinity said. She hesitated for a few seconds, then added, "I dreamed of Alaska and an inukshuk last night." A haunted expression passed over her face, like a drifting cloud crossing the moon in the dark of night. The suddenness sent fear spiraling into him, touching his own body with the chill of death. He swallowed, dread rising yet again.

Maximus frowned. "I also dreamed of an inukshuk." He raked a hand through his hair and grimaced. "Guess we're on the right track, then. I don't believe in coincidences."

"There's no time to waste. Let's get a move on," Alessandro said, hoping the false note of cheer wasn't too obvious in his tone because it was blatantly noticeable to him.

"I think we need a prayer before we go," Trinity said. Her words had surprised both of them, judging by the look his brother shot him.

But the pair stepped up and took her hands. Sparks flew back and forth so hotly between the trio that he wondered that they weren't visible to the naked eye. Energy like he'd never experienced shot through him, pushing the boundaries of his body and mind. He tried to not let it show, but the vibration was strong and it was all he could do not to fall under its sway. Something or someone wanted this union so badly that

January Bain

it pushed hard at him to bow to it. Did the others feel it too? Were they as tuned in and turned on as he was?

"Yes, brother, I feel it. I want to her more than I can say."

"We must stay strong. She needs us to stay strong."

"May this journey be blessed. May we come together with your eternal guidance in search of the holiest of artifacts for the House of Luceres — the Lupus Sanguis Chalice. *Amen.*"

"Amen."

Chapter Eleven

Trinity

Trinity ignored the draw of two huge men who flanked her. Still disbelieving the strange circumstances that had led to this moment, she took out her smartphone and scrolled through websites and cited facts about the place they were about to visit.

"It says that Barrow's name was changed five years ago to City of Utqiaġvik, meaning a place for gathering wild roots. It's a natural hunting place where the peninsula pokes out into the Beaufort Sea. Population of just over four thousand at last count. Forty-six hundred plus miles from Rome. One of the oldest communities, it's been home to whaling ships and is now a science station. The permafrost is thirteen-hundred-feet deep. Yikes, this is even worse!" Her spirits sank with the realization.

"What is it? What's wrong?" Alessandro and Maximus spoke up, their expressions drawn and worried.

"The Polar Night begins on November eighteenth or nineteenth, and the sun remains below the horizon for about sixty-six days. Today is November sixteenth. In two days, the city will be in complete darkness with just an hour or two of hazy twilight. How are we going to see to search?"

"We'll worry about that when we get there, okay? I've had the jet filled with warm clothing and boots. But you should pack toiletries and any personal items you require. Take whatever you want from here. We'll be staying at the King's Inn in town," Alessandro said.

Trinity quickly brought up images of the modern-looking two-storey hotel, trying desperately to keep her mind off the idea of no sunrise in the morning. "The inn looks rather nice. I wonder if they sell teddy polar bears in the gift shop. My sisters would love them."

"We'll buy the *inn*, if that's what you want. Now, get a move on," Maximus said.

"Aye, aye, my captains," she said. If there was ever a time to keep things light, this was it. She'd use all her resources she had, draw on everything in her arsenal to try to keep this ship from floundering off course. To keep herself from drifting out to sea, never to return. She'd read the stories of the Artic winter and its scary legends. She would need her courage now more than ever.

She raced back to the bedroom, ran into the bathroom and packed up shampoo and other necessities for the week-long trip, tossing them haphazardly into a black carry bag she found in the closet.

Pulse pounding, she stopped to view herself in the mirror. Her face was flushed and her hair was all over the damn place. With no time to braid the errant locks, she raised hands that trembled slightly to gather the thick strands into a high ponytail, securing it against her head. That would have to do. Time felt like it was slipping away, moving too quickly, an uncomfortable feeling further heightened by a sense of everything being out of her control. She took a few deep breaths, saying her peace mantra a few times. *Calm and good. Calm and good.*

Another thought struck her, undoing her best efforts to remain serene. Clothes! What was she going to wear? Alessandro had said he was providing warm outerwear, but she couldn't abide the same underwear having to be washed out in the sink every night. In the bedroom she checked the closet and the drawers. There was nothing in her size and nothing looked suitable for one of the coldest cities on Earth. She'd just have to hope that Alessandro had ordered some for her or that she could purchase what she needed in Utqiaġvik. Otherwise, she'd be a sorry sight in a week's time.

There'd be no worries about her libido being out of control by then. Both twins would be turning their noses up at her. Or would they? The electrical current that had bounced between them while they'd all held hands for the prayer was fresh in her mind. *Be careful, Trinity,* her heart warned. *I intend to be, for heaven's sake, I know who I am!*

She sped from the room, the bag clutched in her hand, her focus only on getting to where they had to be. She had a million dollars to pay back if they didn't find the artifact, more than if she counted cards for months and months on end, that was if they would even let her.

The gig was up now, at least for the Glitter Palace casino.

And if they spread the word as to who she was, there would be no gambling in the foreseeable future without undergoing something drastic like plastic surgery. That idea held no appeal whatsoever. Looking in the mirror, not knowing who was looking back? *No, never.* Humble as her circumstances were, at least she knew who she was.

The sound of a supersonic jet flying overhead drew her attention. Probably their ride to Alaska was here, as crazy as that sounded. She couldn't imagine what it must be like to have the kind of resources that called such incredible luxuries at the drop of a hat.

Don't get used to it. One week to see how the top one percent lives, then it's back to reality, kiddo.

Right, Mom.

She sighed, straightened her shoulders and moved to stand in the doorway where the two brothers waited for her thirty feet away at the front entrance.

"Ready?" Maximus asked, holding a black bag of his own, his dark eyes smoldering with the kind of emotion that brought back last night's amazing lovemaking in all its glory. Oh yeah, this was not going to be anything less than the biggest challenge of her life.

She nodded, working to keep her heart rate out of the upper reaches of the hummingbird zone by taking soothing breaths she hoped weren't obvious. What was she thinking? It was certifiable to spent days spent in the company of these two alpha males. Drinking—that was the cure. A bar where she could drown her sorrows and forget this pair existed. That would have to substitute for rolling in the hay at every opportunity with the magnetic Luceres twins.

"You okay, Trinity?" Alessandro asked, a frown creasing the tan flesh between his dark slashes of eyebrows.

"I'm good."

"That you are, *bella signora*," Maximus near purred.

From *sweetheart* spoken like she was a pain in the ass to *beautiful lady* said like he indeed did find her beautiful after last night's romp and made her antsy for some reason. Two sets of dark eyes followed her every movement as she walked across the room to join them. She quirked her mouth into a smile, acknowledging the compliment.

"I hope there's underwear, jeans or shirts in my size onboard or I can buy some in Alaska? I redressed in yesterday's clothes for lack of fresh ones." The words spilled out, mostly to give her something to say.

"What was I thinking?" Alessandro clapped a hand to his forehead. "I meant to have a fresh set of clothing brought to you this morning before breakfast. Yes, I've had choices in your approximate size stowed on the plane. If you need more, we'll have them delivered to our destination."

"Thanks. I'll change on the plane."

Maximus' eyes grew darker, smoldering with the intensity of a thousand suns as he obviously thought about her being naked again.

She drew a shaky breath. *Yeah. Me too.* As soon as she got within touching distance of this pair, she lit up like a damn Christmas tree.

"I need a phone," she said in the no-nonsense tone that she used on her family when they pressed her too far.

The pair shared a look, but Alessandro nodded first and went over to an antique table, opened a drawer and pulled a cell phone out, handing it to her.

"Thank you," she said.

"Okay, let's roll," Alessandro said, giving his brother a significant look.

Maximus nodded and swept his hand toward the door. "After you, *milady*."

His courtly manner took her by surprise, but she couldn't say she hated it. In fact, striding by the pair to join the early morning sunrise just now glinting over the distant hilltops made her feel far too special for her to ever say no to a courtly manner. It was quite the juxtaposition after last night's incredible passion, but better any day than being leered at like was so often the case. Her large breasts in particular tended to get a great deal of attention unless she wore a sack.

My, but that's some fancy jet. The Luceres obviously liked to travel in luxury. The sleek lines of the white aircraft with a slash of red stood out against the Italian countryside.

"The Liberty was one of a dozen produced last year by Bombardier family. Ours was the only one extensively custom made," Alessandro said, standing by her side as she stared at the surreal object parked so grandly on the runway near the villa. She hadn't noticed the awesome convenience last night when they arrived. "We Luceres like a bigger kitchen and bathroom."

"Not to mention a bigger bed to accommodate our size," Maximus said.

She ignored the instant lust his words brought on thinking of them being on that very bed, and instead concentrated on getting one foot in front of the other. She was surrounded by enough testosterone to make her head swim and it wasn't helping.

Near the plane, they were greeted by the captain and one other person, both dressed in black slacks and white shirts. The man wore a red tie with an insignia of a stylized airplane and it was the captain's cap that gave away his position.

"This is Captain Kris Benton and his wife, Ellen Benton. I'd like you to meet Miss Trinity Wells, our guest." Alessandro did the honors.

"Nice to meet you, Miss Wells," the captain said. He was middle-aged, with a trustworthy look of professional pride about him. His wife was a few years younger with a pixie haircut that framed beautiful dark eyes sparkling with good humor.

"Please, call me Trinity."

"Trinity it is."

They shook on it.

"So, you're the young lady I went shopping for last night," Ellen said. She held out her hand for a shake.

"I hope I didn't put you out?" Guilt struck Trinity at the lovely woman being called upon at the last minute to supply her with clothing.

"Not at all. It was rather fun. I was surprised at how stylish sub-zero clothing has become. I just hope most of it fits you."

"Thanks. I'm sure it'll be fine."

"Okay, let's get this show on the road," Maximus said.

They all climbed aboard. Her first reaction was to give a low whistle.

"Well, this doesn't suck," she said to no one in particular.

"Glad you like it. Make yourself comfortable. After takeoff, I'll show you around," Ellen said, gesturing with a hand. The Bensons were easy to like and she instantly trusted them.

"Thanks. I could use some fresh clothes."

"No problem there."

The Bensons settled in the front of the aircraft and the twins escorted her inside to the row of comfortable-looking fine leather recliners that lined the isle.

In no time she was strapped into the most comfortable seat she'd ever sat in, feeling like she was living a daydream. Maximus and Alessandro faced her, their glittering brown eyes focused on her as though she held all the answers to questions she didn't even know yet. *What were they thinking?* Two such handsome, rich men staring at her like she was the finest thing they'd ever seen. But why? They had to have all the women they'd ever need falling all over them. *Weird.* It must have been because they trusted that she would find the artifact. *Only reason any of this makes any sense.*

"Do you suffer from air sickness?" Alessandro asked, his eyes questioning with concern obvious in their creamy brown depths. *Such amazing eyes.* She swallowed and looked away.

"No, but thanks for asking." A gal could too easily fall into the trap that this was more than it appeared. *Keep a grip, Trinity.*

The vibrations of powerful motors rumbled to life and she steeled herself for takeoff. No matter how many times she flew, the sensation of takeoff and landing always gave her pause. But before she knew it, they were moving smoothly down the runway and in a matter of minutes were flying over the countryside.

She turned to look out of the window at the patchwork maze of fields and townships dotting the ground, before they climbed higher and the quilt vanished under a cloud bank. A warmth tingled in her body. Uncertain as to why, she kept her eyes downcast. What was going on? It was as if she wanted to have sex. That was totally unlike her to be thinking about right then. *I mean, I had a great round of lovemaking just last night.* She squeezed her thighs together in efforts to control the lust heating throbbing almost painfully between her legs but it didn't help. But then it went away a few minutes later, making her relax once more.

"Okay, I can help you find some fresh clothing now," Ellen said, at her side.

Trinity unbuckled and got to her feet. "Thanks, that would be great."

She felt two sets of eyes following her as the woman led her into the back of the craft to a series of large boxes stacked neatly against one wall.

Ellen began rummaging through the cartons and came up with a box. She opened it and pulled out a pair of stylish jeans and a pretty red knit sweater. "Would these do?"

Trinity held them against herself, noting they were close to her size. "Perfect if you had some fresh underwear to go with them?"

"I do as it happens."

"Nice." A nice selection of panties and matching bras was located in another container. Trinity chose a set and added them to the clothes she held in her hands.

"You can change in the bathroom. Through that door. I'll catch up with you later. Kris likes me to stay up front with him as I'm his co-pilot."

"Have you been working for the Luceres for long?"

"We started last year. They're great to work for. The pay is the best in the industry, bar none."

"Thanks for this."

"No worries. I was happy to help. You'll find scissors in the vanity to cut off the tags on the clothing."

Ellen left and Trinity headed into the bathroom. Closing the door after being under such scrutiny felt wonderful and she took her time to check out her surroundings before changing.

The only way to describe the scrumptious bathroom that featured a shower stall and huge vanity mirror with drawers that included anything a woman could wish for to groom herself to perfection was awesome. She pulled off her soiled clothing and decided to have a quick shower to freshen up. She took the time to wash her hair again and anoint her skin with a cream that gave off the fragrant of exotic jasmine. Feeling like a princess didn't cut it. She was a queen. *A queen for this day.*

After drying and brushing her hair, she removed the tags and donned the new underwear, admiring the fit as she twirled in front the full-length mirror. She was about to pull on the new jeans when pain struck her mid-section, making her wince and fold her arms over her stomach. Crap. *What is this?* A second wave of pain pushed her to her knees.

She gasped aloud. Was it her appendix? Had it suddenly burst? No, that wasn't it. The anguish was coming from farther down between her thighs now. *Unbelievable.* Her sex was clenching with lust like it had a life of its own. She reached a hand down to touch her pussy through the thin silk of her panties and found she was soaking wet. What the fuck!

The door broke open with a loud sound as it cracked against the wall. Maximus bent down and gathered her into his arms. The sensation of his body being so close to hers rushed over her. More heat instantly followed.

"Are you okay? What happened?"

Alessandro stood over them, his concern for her welfare obvious. He closed the door behind him, giving them privacy.

"I don't know what's wrong," she said, as she reared up and rubbed herself against Maximus. Her nipples begged to be touched, to be sucked. "I've never felt so strangely before. Like I can't help myself."

"She's going into heat. Right now, bro," Maximus said, his voice sounding strained.

"We have to help her," Alessandro said. His eyes smoldered with a leviathan hunger that made her moan as they stared at each other. *Yes.* She knew exactly how they could help her.

"Fuck me. Now!" she said through clenched teeth. Though she couldn't believe she was being so coarse, so demanding, she was right out of control, like someone else had taken over her body completely. And that someone wanted to have sex. *Right. The. Fuck. Now.* And with both strong, powerful, possessive alphas that hovered over her with lust riding high in their eyes.

Chapter Twelve

Maximus

"Are you certain, *bella signora*? Do you want both of us to make love to you? Here and now?"

"Yes, a thousand times yes!" She yanked at his shirt, making the buttons fly off and ping against the walls of the bathroom. She appeared frantic, her scent so enticing it hit him like a firestorm of endorphins, jacking up his own lust level to its highest setting possible. He sent his concerns to Alessandro, holding on to Trinity with all his might.

"We can't worry about the cost to ourselves now. This is meant to be whether we like the timing or not. Her heat must be brought on early because she is who she is. Our Forever Mate."

"I fear you are right."

Maximus tore off Trinity's bra, shredding the lace instantly between his hands. She moaned again and he pulled down her panties, leaving her naked and exposed.

Alessandro moved closer, the fire in his eyes offering no doubt as to how much he wanted to possess Trinity.

He made an instant decision, dimly remembering protocol in his lust to have her again. The hardest words he'd ever have to say in his life awaited him. He said them aloud now before he had the opportunity to renege on what he knew to be right and true.

"You must be next, Alessandro, to ensure that we both imprint on her. If I go now, it will destroy any chance of her being both our mate. To ensure it being done right, I ask this of you. Do you accept?"

"I do." Alessandro needed no second invitation. He pushed Maximus aside and applied his mouth to Trinity's breasts, reaching his hand to the soft junction between her legs that begged to be touched.

Maximus did the second hardest thing of his life.

He stepped back, sat on one of the two chairs in the large room and took a series of deep breaths, frantically trying to steady himself. To keep himself from joining the pair as they had their first, all-important union. But then, everything would be theirs.

Why is her first heat so damn early? In four days, her change would be upon her during the full moon. Then it would have been a given she'd be riding them until they all dropped at some point in the future. But now, it made them vulnerable as hell as a new team And, if this was any indication, watching her writhing right out of control before his very eyes, they were headed for big enough trouble that it would affect the rest of his and Alessandro's life. The stakes had never been higher for finding that damn chalice. His breath froze as he considered the dire consequences that possibly awaited them in the freezing wilds of Alaska.

No. This was too hard for him to watch when his wolf was fighting with him, demanding that he give in and mount her too. *I have to get out of here.*

He leapt to his feet and yanked open the door to the cabin, slamming it shut behind himself. It was only way he could keep from shifting, from possibly exposing himself to the Bensons who were not werewolves but employees of their company.

Chapter Thirteen

Alessandro

Alessandro drew hard on one of Trinity's pebbled pink nipples, eliciting a moan. She was already in the throes of extreme heat and he heard Maximus say that he was taking too much time with foreplay, that it wasn't required or necessary in this case. He needed to offer his knot to stop her punishing pain. If he wouldn't do the right thing, Maximus would step back in, offer his vital assistance.

He growled to let his brother know that would never happen. *"I got this."*

That Trinity was actually in his arms, pliable as a woman could be, was his biggest dream come true. He was so hard now he was certain he was going to pass out from lack of blood and oxygen in his brain. He pulled away from her for just a few seconds to tear his clothes off, uncaring that they were destroyed in the process. She cried out in protest, spurring him to move faster. To claim her body.

He dimly realized that his twin had suddenly departed, leaving the two of them alone. Never had he appreciated his brother more than he did at that exact second. All childhood slights were forgiven. Then his brain shut down, only capable of appreciating the feast that lay so enticingly in front of him. *Trinity in all her glory.*

Naked and harder than he had ever been, he spread her shapely legs, pushing the blunt head of his shaft into her soaking-wet pussy. The welcoming invasion of hard cock into her velvet-like cunt made his new mate mewl with pleasure before she began to ride him for all she was worth.

"Oh my God, that's unbelievably good! Fuck me, Alessandro, fuck me hard. Harder!"

He needed no further enticement. He thrust his hips forward, jerking her onto him with each slam of his body. Their joining was perfect. She arched her back to get him to give her everything he had, her demands searing his skin, making him push in deep as her fingers raked his back. He buried every thick inch of himself into her over and over again, trapping her between himself and the floor.

When his knot began to swell, stretching her, forcing her to lock with him, she only moaned louder. For long delirious minutes, they became one, and it was the most awesome moment of his life. She needed him, needed everything he had. And he gave it freely, wrapping his hands in her hair to demand a kiss from her swollen lips that mimicked her arousal. He fucked her so long and hard that he forgot that his brother was in the next room, awaiting his turn assisting her with her heat if necessary.

No. She's mine for now. The first time for a Forever Mate connected to the twin legend was always done between two consenting adults, not all together. That came later. And if this was indeed what was truly going on, then it had to be done correctly. Then he forgot all about myths and protocols as Trinity's nails raked his back.

A loud passionate growl burst past his lips as he swelled larger still, the new pressure forcing a similar cry from her. The fist-sized knot rubbed against the sensitive nerves locked deep inside her, pushing her into a frenzy of urgent need. Throes that could only be calmed by climaxing over and over until the heat blew itself out.

He grazed her collarbone with his teeth, desperate to mark her, claim her, but he stopped himself. They had to do that together, him and Maximus, to guarantee she would be claimed as their Forever Mate. He held himself in check though he came within a nano second of biting her, filling her with his scent to keep all other wolves away for all time.

When she finally came a few minutes later, his cum filled her pussy to overflowing. She didn't fight it, but squeezed her cunt around his cock, milking his knot. It would act like a balm, easing her tension for a few minutes. But if they truly were her Forever Mates, she would need more in the days to come. She would need both him and his brother to fuck her as much as possible, make her surrender to her raging instinct. Over and over again this pleasure would be shared, cementing them as a trio for all time.

"Are you okay, *bella*?" he asked.

"I—I think so. What the fuck just happened?" Trinity squirmed to escape his arms, like she had just woken from a trance.

"Don't worry, you'll be fine. We'll take good care of you. How are you feeling?"

"Like I've been royally fucked. What the hell was that all about? Did you drug me or something? This can't be normal." She shook her head in denial, her hair brushing over his shoulder causing goosebumps to erupt all over his body. He tamped down his libido, concerned for her welfare his top priority. As it would be from now on.

"I'm going to freshen you up." He got to his feet and bore her into the shower stall, turning the water on.

He carefully cleaned Trinity without protest, washing her soft flesh with care, immersed in enjoying her ample curves. He swept a fragrant squirt of soap over her skin in widening circles, paying special attention to her full breasts. The nipples hardened under his touch—a very satisfying arrangement indeed. Her eyes widened with interest as he slipped his hands lower, massaging her belly.

"You are so lovely," he murmured. The urge to bite her intensified and he'd better hurry this up before the temptation overwhelmed all his defenses.

He cleaned himself quickly, then turned his attention to drying Trinity's sweet little body.

"How are you feeling?" he asked. The extreme need for sex appeared to have abated, her expression calmer.

"Better." She chewed on her bottom lip. "Will that happen again?"

"There is medicine onboard that can ease the cravings. Do you want to try it?"

"I don't know." She eyed him with suspicion. "What are the side effects?"

"Mostly fogginess, a sense of being a bit out of it."

"I need a clear head to help with finding the chalice. Maybe it's not a good idea to take anything that interferes with my thinking processes. And what was *that* for heaven's sake? It was pure lunacy." Her chagrin was obvious, the skin creasing between her eyebrows.

"You were bitten by a wolf back in Vegas. This is the fallout from the event. We call it the heat, and yours is early for some reason. Usually, it happens *after* a female is mated with her partner."

"Oh crap! We didn't use protection!" The horror in her pretty wide-open eyes made him cringe with guilt even while the thought off a son or daughter made his chest swell with pride. Was she also thinking of Maximus? He suspected that it had been a similar case with his twin. But it truly wouldn't make a wit of difference to either of them who impregnated their female. Their DNA was identical.

"Ah, that wasn't really possible. Are you on the pill or anything?" How was he going to explain that the knot prevented the use of condoms quite effectively? They'd burst open—guaranteed. Not that they were needed for disease anyway, quite the opposite, as no werewolf had any worries in that direction.

"Yes, but I don't normally throw myself at men if that's any consolation. I'm more worried about STDs."

"No worries there. We're both a hundred percent healthy. And if any child had developed due to this, I promise you, it will be taken care of. As will you."

"Taken care of! I don't need to be taken care of. My body, my choice."

He didn't think it quite the time to say how little choice she had about the heat, unless she wanted to undergo the terrible pain associated with trying to avoid sex.

"How are you feeling now?" She seemed calmer, her eyes less glazed.

"Better. *Oh my God*, what will the Bensons be thinking? I was so vocal and everything. And your brother? He's going to think less of me."

"Don't worry about them. This part of the plane is well insulated. I doubt they heard anything. Or if they did, they'd never speak of it. And Maximus is fine with this. We both are. It's a twin thing."

She gave him a sceptical look. "I want to get dressed. This is just all so damn crazy. I don't know if I should even be going with both to Alaska, if this is the result. Maybe you can ask the pilot to turn back?"

"Not going to happen. You must go with us. You're meant to be with us."

"The pair of you. Really?" She shook her head. "You both are so out of my league." She was being honest now and it brought him crashing to earth. He had to persuade her of the rightness of all this.

"No, we aren't. We're meant to be together, the three of us. I know it's a lot to take in, but soon you'll see it's the way of it. Give us the time to show you that Maximus and I can take the best care of you. That you need us," he said, using all his powers of persuasion.

"We have to hide our fear for her at all costs, brother."

Chapter Fourteen

Trinity

Trinity wanted desperately to hide her doubts, her chagrin at being so overtaken by lust that she had acted right out of character, leaving a thorn to scratch and prick at her conscious. She'd let it slip that she thought the pair of billionaires were out of her league, but she was going to zip it up from now on. *Keep my dignity intact.* As much as a woman could having thrown herself at two men in less than twenty-four hours. And now, being locked in with them for the foreseeable future, it meant she needed to draw on her legendary willpower to keep herself in check. *I can do this.*

"I've never needed anyone. I go my own way. Make my own decisions," she said, shaking her head.

"How about your family? They affect your decisions, right?"

She shot a glance at Alessandro as she pulled on a pair of jeans and a snug-fitting red sweater. He'd gone out of the bathroom, naked, and got them both something to wear. The shreds of his clothing were all around them, proof positive of how much a clusterfuck this was.

"They do, but that's different."

"How so?" He really looked like he wanted to better understand her, his head cocked sideways to study her with an unabashed intensity in his deep brown eyes. "We're going to be a unit as well. With similar rules that govern family."

"I don't need more rules! I need space to be myself."

"No one is going to take away your personal autonomy, Trinity. We just want to be included. To be part of your life."

"You don't know me! You just want to fuck me, both you and Maximus."

"Don't say it like that. We want a lot more from you than just sex. Not that it wasn't amazing." He drew closer, but she shied away and he was wise enough to let her alone. If he touched her right now, she didn't know what she would do. She raised trembling hands to smooth down the staticky hair that pulling on the sweater had caused.

"Say what you will, but I still think you did something to me. I've never acted like that before — like a slut."

He gave a snort of impatience. "I *never* want to hear you use that word about yourself ever again. This" — he swung a hand wide to encompass things — "was nothing more than you going into heat. It's natural and necessary to bond us."

"You keep saying that. But I don't believe it. There is no such thing as being in heat. That's for animals."

"You have a dual nature now that you've been bitten. In time, you'll see and grow to embrace it."

"Acting like a damn sl—" she stopped herself at the thunderous look that came over his face. "Acting like a fool. I promise you, it won't happen again." And what was this about their bonding? *No need.* When this was over, they'd all go their separate ways. That's how the real world worked.

He came closer, his smile devastating. "Not a problem, Trinity. In Alaska, there will be wide-open spaces and time to show you more of what is to come. I promise you, it will be the time of your life."

Alessandro had a way about him, very different from his brother's. *More reassuring.* He'd calmed her fears, which was no small feat. None of this felt real and it was making the ground beneath her feet shake in an uncomfortable manner. Or maybe that was the fact that they were thousands of feet in the air.

"I guess we joined the Mile High Club in the most exuberant manner possible." She tried for a lighter tone.

His chuckle of good humor was irresistible. "That we did. Now, ready to rejoin the world?"

"Yes, definitely."

He gave her an assessing look. "You look better. Well, beautiful actually."

No man had ever called her beautiful before with such breathtaking honesty. Damn, he made her feel like she was the only woman in his world.

"Aw, thanks. You look very handsome." *Standing in the bathroom of a Lear jet after having wild, passionate, amazing sex with a billionaire after doing his brother last night.* Yeah, this was just all so-o normal.

When they exited the bathroom, her nerves just about got the better of her as she caught sight of Maximus' handsome mug. The extreme intensity in his dark eyes said it all. He wanted to be with her. His keen interest bore into her flesh, making her shiver with anticipation. *No. Not going to happen.* She shook her head defiantly, hoping he'd get the message. *Leave me the heck alone.*

"You okay?" Alessandro asked as he helped her into one of the comfy cushioned loungers masquerading as an airline seat.

She nodded, not trusting herself to speak. *I'm strong and I go my own way.* She said the words a few times. It helped.

"Are you hungry?" he asked a follow-up question.

Just as he inquired, she realized she was famished. Yet again. "Yes, actually. Whatever you've got is fine. I'm not fussy."

Alessandro quickly pulled out a host of hot and cold foods from the serving cart and arranged an impromptu picnic. He filled a china plate for her and arranged it on her chair table before filling one for Maximus and himself.

The ease of being with the brothers was back as they all ate in peace. Quiet classical music she didn't recognize played in the background, further soothing her. When she'd had her fill, she leaned back and smiled at Alessandro as he whisked her empty plate away.

"Thanks. That helped."

"Your wish is my command," he said, a wicked smile lighting his face.

A sudden loud sound made her startle, then a vibration began that unsettled her further. She glanced over at Maximus, who was watching her closely. The intensity of his gaze brought a hot blush to her cheeks.

"Just refueling. It will be over in a few minutes. It will get us to Alaska that much sooner," Maximus said.

"I thought only planes like Air Force One were allowed the convenience. How did you manage it? And why the rush?" The enormity of the expense hit home.

"Money can buy most anything," Maximus said without even so much as a smirk, his mind seeming occupied with weightier matters.

The twins shared a look then as if they could silently correspond. She picked up on something as a few whispered words came of their own bidding into her mind.

"Money can't buy what we most want. She has no idea of the risk. We must protect her and find the chalice before her time."

Confused, uncertain of what she had heard, she sat back and closed her eyes. She needed to rest her mind for a few minutes.

The change in the sounds of the jet's engines woke her. Groggy, she sat up and pushed her hair back from her face. She must have slept for hours because it was dark outside with only landing lights edging the runway visible through the portal. Right, they were in Alaska now which meant early darkness and a Polar Night coming up in a matter of days.

"Hey, sleepyhead. We're here," Alessandro said, affection obvious by his softer tone.

She sat up straighter and glanced over at Maximus. His handsome face appearing in profile while he unbuckled his safety harness struck her anew. She had traveled to Alaska with ancient Roman gods, no doubt of it.

What was she doing here? *It's just a job, Trinity, nothing else. Keep focused on that and it will be fine.*

In a matter of minutes, she was duly dressed in a deep red embroidered fur-lined parka with matching hood and thick winter mittens that near suffocated her in the heat of the plane, but the second she stepped outside were exactly right.

"Wow, this is cold!" she said, clapping her hands together briskly. Each breath she took froze immediately in the frigid air. Her lungs burned, causing her to pull her scarf over her mouth to ease the transition.

An otherworldly sense of being right on the edge of the earth arose as she looked around. The frame buildings with the odd light on inside the dwelling were sparce and few between. All low-lying structures near the runway, they seemed to hug the landscape. Were they in danger of flying off? The strange thought came from nowhere and she dismissed it as a flight of fantasy due to the weather and darkness. *Seasonal affective disorder must be a bitch here.*

Ellen joined her, dressed in a blue parka that appeared just as warm, her pretty face framed by fur. "You'll just be getting used to it and it will be time to head back." She seemed to be perfectly fine with the cold.

"Where's home for you?" Trinity asked.

"Las Vegas, but originally from the Canadian prairies, so this is something I have some experience with. Once you get used to it, it's quite exhilarating."

The sound of distant barking and braying of animals sent chills racing down her spine.

"How do you get around here? Dog sled?" She'd heard about the Iditarod dog sled race held from Anchorage to Nome every winter.

"Yes, and by ski-doo or Bombardier-type vehicles with wider tracks for stability. But you can't beat a good old-fashioned dog sled and team. Still the best way to travel in my opinion." Ellen sounded quite confident about her information, making Trinity more relaxed.

"Will you be staying on?" she asked, praying the answer was in the affirmative. She could use a female friend in this desolate part of the world. They stood to the side of the plane, watching the men unload the multitude of boxes from the plane. They piled the containers into the back of a black SUV with the help of a couple of other males dressed warmly with yellow safety vests over their clothing.

"No, soon as we're unloaded, we're headed to Vegas. We'll be back to pick you up soon as we're called though." Ellen pursed her lips, obviously considering her next words. "With the Luceres' help, I'm sure you'll find what you are looking for. They're both good men, excellent bosses to work for."

"I hope you're right. There's a lot riding on it for me. My family's very fond of my paydays."

"The twins won't leave you in the lurch. I'm certain they'll pay you for your time, no matter what comes of it. They're generous men. And also, I should warn you, wild and unstoppable like all the Luceres clan when they're on the chase. My bet's on you to help tame them."

Her words shocked her and she had no ready answer prepared.

Captain Kris Benton joined them at that moment, making it easier to ignore Ellen's strange words. "Time to go, love. Everything's set."

"Great. Okay, nice to have met you, Trinity. Good luck, hon."

"Thanks, I'll need it." Was there enough good luck in the world to straighten this mess out? And leave her fully intact? She wasn't certain of anything anymore. And watching the pilot and his wife walk away arm in arm gave her a sense of premonition that struck her to the core. A chill crept into her heart that made her swallow hard. Something bad was out there, on the tundra, and its guns were turned in her direction.

Shivering, she kept her glance locked on the outer perimeter of the landscape, or as far as her eyes could see in the starkness of the runway lights. Was that movement? It was so cold, mirages formed just at the outer reaches of her vision as she scanned the area, seeming to wink in and out in a macabre dance. *Get a grip, Trinity*, she chastised herself.

"Let's go, *tesoro*," Maximus called out. The men were waving her over from the SUV, obviously ready to head out.

A pack of wild dogs or wolves howled once more in the night, making her unfreeze. Feet flying across the runway, she arrived breathless at their side, her pulse beating too rapidly.

"Careful, don't be moving too quickly in this cold until you get adjusted," Alessandro warned.

He helped her into the backseat and jumped in behind her, Maximus on her other side. Wedged between the pair, she felt safer. And warmer, as the heater of the vehicle kicked into high gear. One of the men who had helped them unload the plane drove the SUV.

"Where are we staying?" she thought to ask.

"The King's Inn is only a mile away. Be there in a few minutes," Maximus said.

"Right, you told me that earlier." She felt lame drawing attention to herself like that. She of the normally spectacular memory. She rubbed at her forehead. What was going on? Her mind felt foggy, totally incapable of sorting things out as well as she was used to.

"It's the cold, Trinity. It's hard on humans, especially right now with all that's going on with you," Alessandro said.

"I'm fine." She bit off the words. "Don't patronize me, I won't have it."

The excessive anger seemed to come out of nowhere. She felt rather than saw the two brothers look at each other. "*Is she going to be okay?*"

She clasped her hands over her ears, wanting to lock their voices out of her mind.

Chapter Fifteen

Maximus

Alessandro's voice spoke in his mind, drawing his attention. *"I don't know, brother. Maybe the cold is adversely affecting her? She's strong, I am convinced of that. She'll be all right."*

Maximus pressed his lips together. In the past twenty-four hours, everything had changed. Somewhere over the land and sea they had passed by, he had begun to care more than he would like to admit. Lungs filled with the essence of her, watching her sleep, her trust in them obvious — he found her vulnerability overpowering. The last thing he wanted was to have his tiny human upset like this. He wanted to protect her from everything. *Make her life perfect.* But damned if he knew how to do that. He'd never cared about such things ever before and that lack of knowledge was biting him in the ass now. He admired how well

.

Alessandro was handling things, like he had access to a secret roadmap.

"Should we claim her? Would that help?"

"No. I think we should wait. Too much stress on her system as it is."

The SUV stopped in front of their lodgings. One of only a couple of two storey buildings in the town, its warm light spilled outside into the darkness, glowing like a welcoming beacon.

"No matter how angry she gets or out of sort, we must stay calm."

"Of course," he shot back. Who did his twin think he was? A monster? He was all in for keeping her safe, even from herself if need be. The last thing he'd do is upset her, no matter what happened. None of this was her fault.

"I mean no harm, brother."

"I know. But I think our thoughts are intruding on hers. I think we need to keep our talks vocal from now on."

"You may be right." His brother nodded sagely.

"Damn right!"

While the others disembarked from the vehicle, Maximus picked Trinity up in his arms and bore her into the inn, ignoring her instant cries of protest. Before he set her down in the lobby, he kissed her reddened cheeks, aware of the interested glances of the person working behind the reception desk. "Don't worry. We'll take good care of you. You'll have your own suite."

When he set her down, she glared at him. "I don't need coddling. I'm not a child."

"That you aren't, *la mia bella donna*." Him calling her his beautiful woman, followed by his adoring glance of approval, silenced her, though she stood with her arms crossed and lips pursed, waiting.

"May I help you, sir?" the desk clerk asked.

The young man had been watching them with wide-open eyes. He cleared his throat, his Adam's apple nervously ratcheting up and down in his throat as he waited for Maximus to answer his inquiry. The thin young man, not more than twenty-one or twenty-two, had thick dark hair cut short and an olive complexion with dark brown eyes almost black in color. He was dressed in a thick sweater and jeans.

"Yes, we've booked all your available rooms. The Luceres party of three."

At that moment, his brother and the other man came in bearing boxes of the goods necessary for their stay.

"Yes, we have the entire second floor and two of the bottom suites prepared for you. Everything's already paid for, but if you would just sign here, we can get you settled in." The clerk held out a pen and paper and Maximus quickly scribbled his name on it. The nervous young man handed him a set of key cards for the rooms.

"I want a suite on a separate floor," Trinity said, her tone firm.

"Of course. Do you prefer to be on the top or bottom?" he asked, adding a wicked grin for effect. *Time to try a new approach.*

She ignored him though her lips twitched. "Top."

"I've always been partial to cowgirls myself."

"When have you ever even met a cowgirl?" She raised her eyebrows at him as she unzipped her coat. The temperature of the lobby was balmy after the Artic blast at the airport. Not that he or his fellow wolves noticed the cold with their physiology.

"I've been to the Cowgirls Espresso. They all hang out there roping chairs and such." He couldn't resist a smug smile. She wasn't thinking about anything right now but him.

"They do, do they? In a coffee shop? I think you'd have more luck going to watch the Rope for the Crown event held each year at the Plaza in Vegas. You know, if you'd like some authenticity with that expresso?"

"If you two are quite done, we could use a hand over here," Alessandro said.

Maximus had to give his brother credit—he'd waited before interrupting. The other man accompanying them and still in his safety vest looked amused, but remained silent. It didn't mean Maximus wasn't going to continue this vein of charming banter with their mate. If there was ever a time needed to try to keep things on a lighter tone, this was it. *Can't change what happens to a werewolf or a person, only how they cope.* They were words of his father Cesare, the smartest shifter or human he knew. Well, next to his wise sage of a mother.

"I'm partial to authenticity. Which is why I find an Italian scholar so fascinating. To have been hired as a teaching assistant says you have the chops at such a young age."

"I'm hardly fascinating," she said, though he could see that she was pleased.

"You are the most fascinating woman I've ever met."

"Okay, we're right in front of you. Let's get this show on the road." Alessandro the famed peacemaker was about to lose it, by the looks of things.

Maximus retrieved a box from his brother and gave him a wink. *"Just trying to keep things on an even keel, bro."*

"I thought we agreed to stop mind talking?"

"Fine. Let's get *la nostra bella ragazza* settled in her upstairs suite. Everything else stays downstairs."

The three men started up the stairs carrying the boxes marked *Trinity*, leaving the other piled in the lobby with the clerk. There was no elevator in the small Inn, but one set of stairs would be no hindrance. Their mate preceded them, her footsteps light on the steps, the perfumed heat from her body drifting back to keep Maximus hot on her trail.

In the hallway, he set down his load and began opening doors with the key cards provided, letting her choose whichever suite she wanted.

"One that faces the sun or would be if the Polar Night weren't coming," she said walking into a suite that cornered to the east and south.

"Good choice," Alessandro said. "I think I'll choose the one directly below this one, if it's available."

Maximus had wanted those rooms knowing she was just above him, but his brother had spoken first. He would have paid any price to have them if they had already been occupied. Of course, it didn't mean he'd be staying downstairs. He was certain he could manage to find his way back into Trinity's bed in record time. The heat had hit her once—it was certain to hit again. And who was he to keep her from experiencing incredible, amazing, sweet pleasure? Nothing could describe how wonderful their lovemaking had been, and if she accepted them as her Forever Mates, all bets were off as to how perfect it was going to become. They'd blow the ceiling off this joint.

They piled her boxes on a couple of chairs. The time had come. He handed Trinity her key card, their fingers touching in the process, sending sparks through him. Her too, by the look of intensity in her beautiful blue eyes. With her fairish hair escaping into tendrils around her gorgeous face, she looked otherworldly in the light of the old-fashioned lamps that gave off a soft glow. He wanted nothing more than to peel all those clothes off her and demonstrate his need for her, even with the others looking on. But it wouldn't be right and he kept himself in check by the barest of threads.

"Sleep well, Trinity. Call us when you wake up and we'll have breakfast together," Alessandro said.

"And if you need anything, anything at all, just call me. I'm a light sleeper," he said, cupping her cheek for an instant before turning and exiting the room. The look in her eyes would keep him awake this night, thinking of what they'd already experienced and what was yet to be.

Chapter Sixteen

Alessandro

"What was all that about, Maximus? If you think you're going to horn in and become her go-to guy, I'm telling you I'm putting a stop to it right now." Alessandro poured two half-glasses of the finest single malt whiskey ever produced, Dalmore 62, the favored drink of their pack, and that they bought by the truck load. He handed one to his twin.

"I'm not trying to become her 'go-to guy' as you put it. Just trying to do my part to keep her calm. You're not the only one capable of being there for her. Did you forget how I stepped aside to let you and her begin the bonding process?" Maximus took a gulp of the liquor, raking one hand through his short hair.

The reminder shut Alessandro up. Yes, he was being ungrateful. He'd never seen his brother be into self-sacrificing before. It was just that things had shifted so far from his normal existence in the past twenty-four hours that he was out of sorts. He wanted, no *needed* to help Trinity so much, to make her life perfect, and he had no idea how to do that right now. And Maximus had so smoothly charmed her, making him feel less than.

"We need to run. Work off this stress. And it will give us a chance to see the landscape firsthand. Are you up for it?"

"You know it, brother. But what about Trinity?"

"We'll make this fast."

They both polished off the whiskey, set their glasses down and re-dressed in their parkas. A run on the wilds of the Alaskan tundra. That would help him gain perspective, and also get a glimpse of what they were facing. How were they going to find the exact spot needed to locate the priceless chalice? How many inukshuk littered the landscape?

They exited the inn together and strode up to the SUV parked and ready as ordered near the entrance. Before they'd left Rome, Alessandro had studied maps of the area and knew where they were headed.

"Want to drive?" he asked, trying to make up for his aggression earlier.

"You know it."

Maximus found the keys over the visor and threw the vehicle into drive before hitting the gas and racing off down the road. Exhaust from the vehicle billowed behind them in the extreme temperature. A few minutes later, a few miles from the town, his brother parked the SUV, turning off the motor.

When they disembarked, leaving their clothes behind, he glanced up at the sky, awed into silence. The famed Aurora Borealis or Northern Lights were in full glory. A wild display of ever-changing hues of green swirled above them, creating an unusual portal that felt like it could lead right into the heavens. The magical vision had a down-to-earth explanation, of course — magnetic storm energy. But at the moment, it seemed to portend something more. What exactly, Alessandro wasn't certain. But under his scholarly cloak, he knew himself to be swayed by fantasy, far more than his pragmatic twin who enjoyed teasing him about it on occasion.

"The dragons are dancing tonight," Maximus said with a look, choosing to offer the Japanese myth about the magnificent lights. "Best be careful."

"Let's get this done. I don't like leaving Trinity alone for long." His brother might be able to play at being level-headed, but Alessandro felt the seriousness of their precarious position. It was obvious now that both of them were falling, and falling hard, for the tiny female asleep back at the inn. *Each hour, each minute, precious. No time to waste.* His very soul seemed to have a clock ticking ever more loudly and he worried that it would explode if things didn't go well.

In mere seconds, they were through the closest dimension of the eleven available. *M-theory got that reality down pat.* Then it was back to the best one, and they raced across the frozen ground, fur frosting over from the moisture in the air.

The night seemed too silent while their running leaps ate up the distance, as if the whole world held its collective breath.

"Where are the wolves we heard earlier, bro?"

"I don't know."

How would they find the spot they had to locate in a sea of frozen ice? What if the correct inukshuk no longer existed? Buried under ice and snow? Alessandro was too worried, even as wolf, to enjoy the run. Finally, a stone man rose in the distance and the pair stopped to sniff out the snow-covered area at its base, checking for clues. It was a recent rebuild, leaving traces of modern men. *No scent of wolf.* Either the artifact was buried very deeply — unlikely on such a difficult-to-unearth landscape — or it wasn't at the spot. They would need a guide, an elder, someone whose ancestors had lived in the area for eons. And someone they could trust to keep their secret.

They turned in tandem a few miles out, both seeming to come to the same conclusion at the same moment, and made a full circle back to their waiting vehicle.

Re-dressing, they headed back to the inn. The run had only released pent-up energy, not satisfied on any other level. The worst part was that it might be the last one they could manage until whatever waited them was over. Or the last one ever as they were now, complete and whole, their mate alive and needing them.

Alessandro turned his mind away from the yawning abyss that had captured too many unsuspecting souls, knowing the importance of staying strong, staying focused. He couldn't afford to think that far ahead.

The inn was quiet when they entered. They both needed a few hours of rest if that was possible before the trials of the coming day.

In his room, Alessandro lay down on the bed, fully dressed, listening. The soft, rhythmic sounds of Trinity breathing in the bed just above him reassured him and he closed his eyes. In seconds, he was fast asleep.

Something woke him a short while later, and he was instantly alert, searching the room with furtive glances for the reason. Nothing appeared disturbed. He jumped to his feet and crossed to the window, pulling the heavy drapes aside to look out into the shadowy darkness. Several pairs of glittering eyes watched the inn, about a hundred yards away. Heads low to the ground, it was a pack of wolves, their white fur blending into the snowpack.

He growled deep in his throat, alerting them to the fact he was there, watching them. The stood for a moment longer, then turned and melted into the distance.

Who are they? He sensed their supernaturalness. An unknown pack, living so high in the Artic, they must have fallen under the radar. Not all packs knew one another — no complete registry of werewolves existed, beyond the one the Luceres created of their own ancestry. And meeting a new pack could be very dangerous if they took umbrage to him and Maximus invading their territory.

"Pack alert. See them, brother?"

No answer. Maximus must still be asleep. He checked the time. Five a.m. Early, but he knew he wouldn't be getting back to sleep anytime soon. He headed for the shower, shedding his clothes on the way. It was time to send out inquiries for an elder who might assist them, give them knowledge on the timelines and legends of ancient inukshuk.

Twenty minutes later, he entered the small dinning room whose chalkboard offered an early bird breakfast special of bacon, eggs and toast. The room's décor was simple, well-built sturdy furniture that included an interesting oil painting of a whaling ship, an inukshuk, and a pack of white wolves. There was one other patron sitting at a table for four in the restaurant that had room for about twenty people in total. He stopped himself from going over and inspecting the picture more closely, knowing he was being watched.

"Good morning," he said with a nod at the old man. It was too small a town to ignore a person in the same room, unlike a larger city where one minded their own damn business at all times. The elderly man surveyed him with ancient eyes that appeared to bore right into his soul. His high-cheekboned and weathered face was a series of deep wrinkles etched into tan skin, his thick white hair an untidy thatch. His brown bibbed canvas clothing was worn overtop a dark plaid flannel shirt. He wore leather moccasins on his feet, though not the outdoor kind.

The man made a polite gesture with his hand. "Come, Alessandro of the House of Luceres, sit with me. We have things to discuss. My granddaughter Mae will bring us breakfast when it's ready."

Alessandro took the offered hand. The man had a strong grip for a man looking to be in his eighties if he was a day. It was then he caught the whiff of supernaturalness emanating from the man. Was he werewolf or something else? He'd never smelled that particular odor before and it cautioned him, though it meant the man also knew of his heritage and yet sat here waiting to speak with him.

"And you are?" he asked, sitting and joining the old man.

"Tikaani. It means ancient warrior."

"How do you know of my affiliation to the House of Luceres?"

The man gave a bark of satisfaction. "You think just because we live in the high Artic, we know nothing of the other world that you bring into our village? We have the internet and big-screen TVs. Some youngsters even play poker online." He shook head. "Idiots. No money in that beggared scheme. Word of your arrival on a private jet has spread everywhere. Your family is well known in the Vegas casino trade, is it not?"

"Touché. You have lived here all your life?"

A young woman in jeans and a bright red sweatshirt came into the room at that moment, carrying a glass carafe that gave off the heady fragrance of fresh-brewed caffeine. Coming over to their table, she nodded at Alessandro. "Coffee, sir?"

"Please."

She turned over one of the cups that sat on the table and poured it full of the steaming substance that would set his day off right. Why did he get the distinct feeling it was going to be all downhill from here? He pushed back at the thought, preferring a neutral position until things revealed themselves.

"Cream?" She went to fish out a couple of creamers from a pocket in her apron. She couldn't be more than twenty-one and resembled the young clerk from the night before. Her long black hair was pulled back in a ponytail, and her face was free of any makeup.

He waved her away. "No, black is fine and I'll have your breakfast special."

"Already cooking. More coffee, Grandfather?"

"Yes."

She filled his cup and left a fistful of creamers on the wooden tabletop. "I'll be back in a jiff with your meals."

"Why are you here among us, Alessandro?" the older man asked.

He took a moment to take a gulp of coffee, needing a moment to find the correct words. How much to tell the old man? And was this the elder they needed who would know the history of the area?

"It's been a long journey that has brought my brother Maximus and I to this part of the world."

"And a young woman as well. No?"

He had nothing to lose in trusting the man. Time was too short now to play games. *Just a couple of days until the full moon and the change.* The thought sent an icicle of fear into him. "Yes, Trinity Wells. We are looking for something, the three of us. Something of great value to the House of Luceres."

"But first I will tell you a story. Have you heard of the Tornits, great hairy beasts that roam the Land of the Midnight Sun?"

Alessandro shook his head, drinking more of the delicious coffee.

"There is a legend that they seek the *Aunâk Kajottak*."

"Blood cup," Alessandro said.

"You are a learned man, my friend. Not many would know our language well enough to translate. You come seeking to acquire it? Many have come on a similar journey. All have failed."

Doubts crept in. Why would they think they could be any luckier than those who had come before? Finding the blood chalice was the longest shot he'd ever played, and the old man who knew so much, who was so much more than he was saying, was warning him of the futility of his journey.

"I need your help, Tikaani. The woman we brought with us, Trinity Wells, she is sick and not of her own making, and she needs our help."

"You care about this woman?"

"I do, very much."

"It is a dangerous path you seek. The woman may die anyway."

"It doesn't matter. I will give my life for hers." And at that moment, he knew it to be true. Trinity was meant to be their Forever Mate. Everything about her called to him. To his brother Maximus as well. It was just a matter of making her see that.

Chapter Seventeen

Trinity

Trinity awoke slowly, as if from the deepest of comas. *Where am I?* The room was unfamiliar. She rubbed her forehead with fingers that trembled uncontrollably. What was happening to her? The bite on her arm itched and she dug her fingernails into the tender flesh to try to stop the sensation. It only made it worse and she stumbled from the bed in an effort to stop thinking about it.

She went to the window and yanked at the drawstring that pulled the drapes. A vast snowy landscape stared back at her, hazy in the dawn of a new day. Steam was rising from the various buildings that littered the area, straight up in the air, which meant no wind. *Right.* She was in Alaska. And she had a job to do. She'd best get her head around to facing front with a million dollars at stake.

She hurried into the shower as if the hounds of hell were on her heels and stood under the cold, driving water to clear her mind until she began to shiver. Briskly drying off, she hauled on fresh underwear, clean jeans and a warm blue sweater with a white snowflake motif.

Hunger hit hard as she was pulling on a pair of flat-heeled boots, making her bend over in pain. Holding her stomach, she slowly straightened up. *Gotta get something to eat. This is crazy.*

She hurried down the one flight of stairs and headed into the room marked *The King's Restaurant*. It was nearly empty, with just Alessandro sitting at a table with an elderly man. She approached the two, suddenly feeling shy.

Alessandro caught sight of her and stood to greet her. He gave her the Italian old-world greeting of double cheek kisses, bringing a smile to her face.

"Morning, Trinity. You look lovely. You must be starved. Sit, my food just arrived. I'll order another. Please."

Like he knew she couldn't wait, he seated her and pushed his full plate in front of her. The fragrance of smoky bacon and buttery eggs hit her hard and she was challenged not to down it all in mere seconds.

But first she needed to be polite. "I'm Trinity Wells, sir." She held out her hand to the older man who sat across from her and watched her with a solemnness that bespoke of wisdom and patience far beyond what she knew herself to be capable of. He held on to her hand for a few seconds, long enough to make her blush with nervousness.

"It is an honor to meet you, Miss Wells. Please, call me Tikaani. It's not every day I hear a man say he will die for a woman. You are worth that sacrifice, I see."

Confused, she swallowed. Who did he mean? She looked at Alessandro, sitting on her righthand side, noting his solemn expression. Did he mean that Alessandro had said such a thing? They locked glances and she knew. *Yes.* The elder meant *this* man. He had said it out loud recently. *But he hardly knows me. Why would he say such a thing?*

"Eat, *bella*. You must be starved. And we have a long day ahead of us. You must keep up your strength. The cold will zap you otherwise."

"Your man is right. You must eat well. And you must stay close to each other. Danger lurks for the unwary here," the elder said.

"I don't want to take your food away," she protested. The old man's words concerned her. *What danger?*

"Not to worry, here comes another plateful."

A waitress was indeed hurrying across the floor carrying another plate of food in her hands. She handed it off to Alessandro.

"If you need more, just ask," she said. "You're all up from the south, right?"

The young woman looked so full of excitement with her dark eyes flashing intense interest in her customers that Trinity broke out in a huge smile. "We are. Your food smells delicious, by the way."

"Thanks. Go ahead and eat. I'll be by again." She hurried away.

Trinity needed no other enticement but attacked her food with relish. In short order her plate was empty, Alessandro's and the elder's in the same state.

"We will have pie now," the elder said with relish.

"Pie for breakfast?" she asked in a teasing tone. "You are my kind of man, sir." She couldn't imagine calling him by his first name. Elders deserved the utmost respect.

He smiled, his wrinkled face lighting up as if he knew what she was thinking. "You know never to refuse the offer of dessert, Miss Wells." He raised his voice that was still surprisingly strong, an innate authority underling it. "Granddaughter, bring us your best homemade pie to share."

"Where is Maximus this morning?" she asked his brother while they waited for the offering to arrive.

"Speaking of the devil," Alessandro said with a smile. "Here he is now."

Maximus strode over to their table bringing the exhilarating and fresh scents of the outside with him. He looked good, still dressed in his parka though he had unzipped it, exposing his well-defined pecs outlined by a black cashmere sweater. A light scruff of dark shadow on his chin showed for the first time. It emphasized his lantern jaw while his thick dark hair was tousled in a charming manner, making her want to run her fingers through it.

Now that she had eaten, she noticed both men with far more alacrity. Alessandro looked just as yummy with his long-sleeved black T-shirt stretched tight over his broad shoulders tapering to a trim waistline, his strong thighs encased in dark washed jeans.

The Luceres twins were far more than she had ever bargained for, but oh, how they enticed her, these warriors in their prime. There was no way a hot-blooded woman could choose between them. They were both so perfect, each in their own way.

"Just in time for pie, bro," Alessandro said, gesturing at the last chair at their table beside Sir Tikaani, the name she now attached to the elderly man. She would never forget him, she was certain, as long as she lived, he had made that much of an impression.

"Maximus, I'd like you to meet Sir Tikaani," Trinity said, deciding to take it upon herself. The smile that lit up the elder's face at her address of him was all the thanks she needed.

"You come from the land of Joshua trees shaped as men, Maximus?" Sir Tikaani asked, his keen dark eyes assessing their new table mate.

"I do. My family has deep roots in the desert. As I imagine yours does in the far north."

"Yes. The land of supernatural men made of rock and stone to mark the landscape. Our people call them inunnguaq, and you call them inukshuk."

"We come seeking one. A very special one." Maximus' eyes glittered with intent, and she felt his heightened alertness, though he tried to hide it by drinking his coffee.

"One that may lead you to the Aunâk Kajottak, yes?"

"The Aunâk Kajottak is another name for the object we seek?" she inquired, fairly certain of the answer. Alessandro took her hand and squeezed it gently, making her entire body step up and take note. It felt nice, to hold hands with him, though she was certain it would be just as nice with Maximus. The twin thing was not so brand new anymore, but was developing at lightning speed into something much, much more. Where it would lead to, she had no idea, but she wanted to be there for it.

"I have already shared with your brother that you have arrived in a dangerous land, filled with old ghosts and ancient legends. That the journey to search for what you require on this barren, brutal landscape will be taxing. More than you know. Aw, the pie has arrived. Thank you, granddaughter. We'll talk more after we eat."

The warm pie gave off a wonderous scent of apples and cinnamon and made her mouth water. The lovely girl who set it down in the center of the table for everyone to share blessed them with another beaming smile before scurrying away. In no time flat, the pie had disappeared, aided by cups of fragrant, strong coffee laced with dollops of cream and whiskey which the elder produced in a battered copper hipflask from his jacket pocket.

"One must enjoy their vices when time permits," he said, before raising his mug. "A toast to the most intriguing trio I have had the pleasure of meeting in my lifetime. May you find what you seek." He nodded like he had made a momentous decision.

Trinity had never felt so embraced before, and the rare moment spoke to her on a deeper level. She shared an approving look with the old man, knowing her smile was genuine, as was his.

"Now, down to business." The elder pulled out a threadbare, hand-drawn map that he carefully unfolded and spread out on the tabletop after the others pushed their plates to the side. "There is a cairn built in the center of the Alaskan vortex that has mysterious powers. People have been known to vanish from the face of the earth at that location. For hundreds of years, there have been whispers of a blood cup hidden there. That it will take strong men to reveal its power. But I warn you it is an arduous journey, over fifty miles by dog sled, the only way in, and you must take the woman with you. Too much danger lurks for her here."

"May we have this map?" Maximus asked with a scowl on his face, obviously concerned about the warning. Was he worried for her if she stayed in town or because the journey would be so arduous? "I promise to keep it safe."

"May I ask why you have not retrieved the artifact for yourself?" Alessandro asked.

"The artifact belonged to your ancestors, did it not? It wasn't ours to claim. But the map has a certain sentimental value." The old man nodded and settled back in his chair.

"That settles it then. Thank you, sir, for your help," Alessandro said. "If we can ever repay you in kind, just ask. Anything at all, I will see it done."

"I may take you up on that offer one day soon. My granddaughter wants to see the south and I fear for her. With someone to look over her, I would be comforted."

"Anytime, she would be most welcomed to visit us and stay as long as she wants," Alessandro said.

"I would love to show her around," Trinity added. She knew all too well what it was like to be feeling without roots when visiting a new place. She felt it here, felt the disturbance to the mind and body that came from the unknown. *From unexpected change.* The least she could do was help another over the hardest bit. "It would be my pleasure."

"Thank you," Sir Tikaani said, his dark eyes tinged by sadness. "I will pray that the journey is fruitful for all of you and that you are blessed with a long life, Miss

Wells. It is in the creator's hands now to rescue you. If you find what you seek, remember that blood is life."

She stilled, his warning freezing her breath. The depth of understanding in the ancient man filled her with a longing to know more. To see everything as it really was, not be hampered by the blinders and limits of human understanding. She sat up straighter. What was it about this part of the world that she was becoming so maudlin? She was normally considered a go-getter, a woman who didn't like to sit still and ponder.

She scratched impatiently at her arm, the image of a huge gray wolf running across the tundra focusing her mind. He was coming for her! She blinked, trying to wish it away. The vision was a portend of danger, she knew with dead certainty, her meal roiling in her stomach.

She pushed against Maximus to let him know she wanted up. "I need to use the restroom," she said by explanation. "Excuse me."

He moved to let her exit, and she rushed from the restaurant and raced up the stairs to her room. She just made the bathroom when she began to vomit. In mere seconds, she emptied her body of breakfast, her stomach heaving.

She moved over to the sink and washed her mouth out with handfuls of water. What was the matter with her? All that good food had gone to waste now. One moment it was fine, the next she was throwing up? But dread still clung to her, sensing her life was in a state of flux that threatened to swamp her if she didn't keep it together. *What was it that Vincent Van Gogh said? There is peace even in the storm. Right, I just need to find that place and hold on tight.*

Chapter Eighteen

Maximus

"I hope your woman will be all right," the elder said as he got up. "I will leave you now. For the best sled and dogs, see my nephew Amaqjuaq. He'll set you up. You can find him at Barrow's General Store. Tell him I sent you."

"I'm certain we will meet again," Maximus said, extending his hand to the elder. "Thank you for your help."

"Just keep that young lady safe. She's special, but you already know that."

Maximus bristled, but kept himself in check. Alessandro bid the man farewell and they watched him leave, the bounce in his step defying his age.

"What is he? One of us?" Alessandro asked, his expression pensive.

Maximus shrugged. "If he is, he's one of the ancients. I sense a different animal though. Maybe even a polar bear totem."

"Really? I'd only ever heard rumors of their existence."

"No more time for this—we need to be off. I'm going up to check on Trinity."

"I'm coming with you," Alessandro said, matching him step for step as they hurried up the stairs. Maximus knocked on her door, masking his concern.

The door opened almost instantly, revealing Trinity dressed in all her outside gear.

"Good. I thought maybe you weren't feeling well?"

"I'm fine. Let's go."

Her answer was a bit short. Was she all right? Or just putting on a brave face? His bet would be on the latter, giving him one more reason to admire her.

"We're headed to the Barrow's General Store to hire a dog team and sled."

"How far can they travel in one day?"

Her question set off a clock ticking down in his mind. With the full moon only two days away and the Polar Night closing in, would they make it in time? He couldn't imagine the Lupus Sanguis Chalice not being there. That would be too cruel. And his mind refused to consider the ramifications of any other outcome than success. *No. Best to keep moving forward.*

"Depends on the terrain. Forty or fifty miles a day. And it's a hundred miles to the inukshuk. Of course, we'll get the fastest, strongest dog team possible."

"Going to be a tough hike for the dogs," Alessandro mused. "What if they don't—you know—take to us?"

Maximus shrugged if off, hoping their wolf nature wouldn't be too much of a factor for the wilder dogs of the north country. Southern canines didn't usually take to werewolves, mostly running away or cringing in fear. "I'm sure the team must be used to that. The Innuit have traveled vast distances for millennia. The only one affected is likely to be Trinity, with her changing nature. But we'll be there to be her eyes and ears."

"I'll be fine," Trinity said, her mouth pursed in disapproval. All Maximus wanted to do was to kiss those pretty pouty lips and it was the one thing he should not do in her current mood. He didn't need a relationship coach to realize that.

"You grab your gear, Alessandro. Meet us in the lobby," he instructed.

The three of them trooped down the stairs.

"Can I get you anything?" Maximus asked Trinity while they waited near the reception desk. No one else was in the lobby because everyone else had checked out. He'd ordered the clerk to take no more bookings so that when they got back, they would have the entire inn to themselves. He ignored the voice that taunted, *If you get back from your trip.* There were some things that money couldn't buy, and this was one of those rarest situations.

She shook her head.

"How about a stuffed bear?" He added a charming smile. With the hormones charging through her system as her body worked to prepare for the change, she had to be in turmoil.

She looked at the display and went over to touch one of the plush white bears festooned with a bright red bow round its neck.

"They are nice. Not sure which ones my sisters would prefer. They're pretty fussy."

"No need to decide now. I bought them all. And this inn too, in fact. It will become a permanent home for the Luceres in the north. Though I'm not sure how many will want to leave the heat of Vegas everyone's so partial to."

"I can't imagine what it must be like to just buy whatever you want. That must be kind of awesome."

"Some things, the most important things, can't be bought. Like family, honor and love."

"True." She looked at him then, hitting him with those gorgeous blue eyes of hers, the crystal clearness of the irises stirring something so deep in him that it hurt to breathe.

"Sorry I took so long." Alessandro hurried up, his heavy polar pack boots resounding on the floor.

"Let's go," Maximus said, zipping up his parka before they escorted Trinity out to the SUV that he'd left running to keep warm for her.

It was a short trip to the Barrow's General Store. They all piled out again when he parked in front of the establishment, the lone vehicle on the lot. Inside the low-riding steel building, he gave a quick look around. Shelves of everything imaginable filled the vast space. From snowmobiles to baked bread, it was all available, for a price.

A young woman looked up from her position at one of the two checkout tills, a narrow white roll of paper clutched in one hand suggesting she was replacing the tape on the cash register. "Can I help you?" she asked, her eyes wide and rounded by curiosity.

"We're looking for Amaqjuaq. His uncle said he would be here?" Maximus inquired.

"Yes, he's expecting you. Just head to the back, through those doors." She pointed the way, never taking her eyes of the three of them.

"Thank you."

She nodded, then blushed, seeming to remember her manners. Dropping her head, she resumed her task.

They strode down the aisle and he pushed through the saloon-type door, the others following him. If he'd thought the front was filled with goods, the back warehouse was even more crowded.

"Hello, anyone there?" Maximus half-shouted.

A burly young man came into view, a scowl on his broad face as he observed them with dark eyes. He was built like a linebacker with a thick thatch of black hair, his acne-scarred cheeks fleshy above his thick neck. He nodded once. Maximus knew instantly he was a northern wolf. And, actually, that made the transaction easier. It would mean the dogs were used to being controlled by shifters. *Used to the domination and unlikely to kick up a fuss.*

"You must be the guys my uncle said were on their way over. Looking for some dogs, are you? I warn you, it's going to cost you. Though I hear you already bought the King's Inn, so that should be no problem, right?" The young man rubbed the palms of his hands together.

Was his attitude due to jealousy or to their being from different packs? Not all werewolves were as rich as the Luceres, by any means. Whatever, Maximus didn't have time to sort that out. "No problem at all. We'll pay for the best you have. Our destination is a two-hundred-miles round trip. Going to need provisions for the team as well. Can you provide them?"

"Sure, we got lots of frozen fish. Going to cost extra."

"Wouldn't have it any other way." Maximus pulled two wrapped stacks of one-hundred-dollar bills from his pocket worth twenty thousand dollars. "Cash or credit card?"

"Cash works. Eight grand for the easy rider sled and full team. Five hundred for the fish."

"Okay if I buy the sled and team, then leave them with you between trips up north?" Maximus handed over the money.

"No problem there. Upkeep's going to cost."

He counted off an additional five thousand. "That enough for the winter? You'll have use of the team, of course, when we're not here. Just expect them to be treated well."

The younger man bristled, but the cash plus the generous tip he held in his hand tempered him. "I treat my dogs well."

"Good. That's all I ask."

"How soon will everything be ready? Supplies on board for the dogs?"

"Already done and waiting out back. My uncle said speed was of the utmost importance."

"Our bags are in our vehicle. We'll drive around and you can help us load them." The last was a statement, not a question. The man had been amply paid already.

He gave another slight nod, his expression still wary.

"The lady can wait here with me, if she wants." His dark eyes glittered and Maximus growled, letting him to know to back off. The cur spun on his heels and headed toward the man door, presumably to go and wait for them.

He took Trinity's arm and led her back through the store and outside. She started shivering soon as they left the warm building and hit the frigid air. He wanted badly to protect her from any discomfort and had made it his mission to learn all he could to prevent that from happening.

"I've brought warm coverings for the sled and hand and foot warmers for your gloves and feet. I promise to keep you warm. Day and night, you have my word."

"Thank you. It was just so warm in the store compared to outside, it's a bit of a shock. I'll climatize soon. I'm considered quite sturdy in my family. The one voted most likely to go the distance, no matter what's thrown at me." She gave him a sweet smile to punctuate her remarks.

Her courage astounded him. He could only imagine what a strong mate she was going to be. Her loyalty was beyond question to family, even doing things it was obvious she would not do with other choices being offered. He began to pray like he had never prayed before. *Please let her live. I'll do anything you ask, Lord, if you let Trinity live.* He hid all the worry inside, not wanting to frighten her. "You are one of a kind, *tesoro*. I don't believe I've ever met anyone quite like you before."

"We both promise to keep you safe," Alessandro spoke up, his voice steady and certain. They would all need each other, now more then ever.

"Of that I have no question," she said, her answer warming him.

He drove them around to the back of the store, parking the SUV beside a large fenced-in compound. Dogs were barking and he spotted the nephew dealing with a team already in traces waiting to be driven away, as promised.

It was a large sled being pulled behind the twelve huskies in their prime, with enough room to make a warm bed for Trinity and carry all their supplies, plus room for one of them to stand while the other sat behind their mate. Exactly what was required.

In short order, the young man helped them load the sled with their camping supplies, warm bedding and extra clothes. After Trinity was given the best spot, snuggled under a pile of Hudson Bay wool blankets with their distinctive red, green, navy and yellow end stripes, he waited for Alessandro to get aboard. When his brother was secure, Maximus took up the reins, giving the command, "Mush!"

The team was responsive, eager to be off, and the trio was whisked from the yards. Trinity waved goodbye to Amaqjuaq, making Maximus grind his teeth. He hid his chagrin and encouraged the dogs to better speed, the wind whistling by them as they found the trail that led out of town in the dim twilight of the morning. It had been pointed out to him by the precious map securely zipped in his jacket pocket.

The moment was exhilarating, a time travel adventure come to life, and he basked in the sense of control that moving the well-built sled smoothly over the ice and snow of the ancient tundra gave him. Not since he'd read Michener's *Alaska* had he better understood the lure of the northernmost reaches. It called to a man's spirit, set him on a course of self-improvement, knowing he would be tested like nothing that had come before.

He relished the chance to prove himself alpha. "*Step up and be strong, boy.*" Words from his father Cesare centered him and he adopted it as his mantra as the miles flew by, each cairn dotting the landscape bringing them ever closer to the one that mattered. The one had to would save their mate.

Chapter Nineteen

Alessandro

The gunmetal gray-blue sky, hazy sun low on the horizon and soon to disappear entirely for weeks on end, caused Alessandro to reflect on what he had read about Alaska. According to geological experts, a billion years ago, it had been a small protuberance jutting out from the northwest corner and its rootstock had always been permanently attached to primordial North America. Sometimes drifting into tropical climes, it would have been difficult to predict its final resting place. *Miraculous, really.* Now, they needed one more miracle from this desolate land of hidden treasure. *Finding the chalice.* Snuggled in the sled behind Trinity, he picked up on Maximus' prayers, and added his own to send out into the universe. To ask for mercy.

The miles flew by in contemplative reflection, the dogs responding well to his brother's handling. He had to remind himself, breathing in the intoxicating scent of their future mate, that they still stood a chance of finding the precious artifact in time. Surely fate wouldn't allow them to get this close, then turn it into a fruitless search? No one could be that cruel.

For so much of his adulthood, the wolf had warred with the scholar, but now the different parts of his personality were meshing. His knowledge would be the catalyst for saving their mate, he had to be certain of that. Or be doomed, a spirit drifting through time. Surely that could not be the final outcomes? Perhaps the reality of endless night closing in preyed too heavily on his mind, the reason behind his maudlin thoughts. He shook his head. Now more than ever he had to rely on his wolf's strength to pull them through.

They stopped at midday, near one of the cairns marked on the map, to give the dogs a needed rest and to have a quick meal. The cold was not the place to be concerned about calories.

"We'll have a hot meal tonight before bed, but for now a thermos of hot coffee and protein bars will have to do," Maximus said.

Alessandro dolled out the food, knowing the dogs had to wait for their fish until last stop, as that was best for their constitutions, according to the instructions imparted by a host of knowledgeable websites and by their trainer.

He poured the steaming coffee then handed Trinity the cup. The three of them sat on folding campstools unloaded from the sled.

"Thanks," she said and took an appreciative sip. She could not look more lovely with her cheeks pinked by the cold. "You know, I could get use to this mode of travel and all the attention. Never been spoiled in my life before. Kind of cool."

"Stay with us and this will become your new norm," Alessandro said, keeping his tone neutral.

"Stay with you. You mean like — from now on?" she looked at him with a quizzical expression. She looked so darn pretty with the ruff of white fur framing her face, one errant curl escaping across her forehead, that it was all he could do not to pull her into his arms and make love her over and over again.

"Yes, that's exactly what I mean. We'll become the newest three musketeers, joined together as one. *Un pour tous, tous pour un.* One for all, all for one."

"I like that. One for all, all for one," Maximus said, saluting with his mug of hot coffee.

Trinity looked from one of them to the other, shaking her head. "I've never met a pair like you. But I must admit, we're firing on all cylinders, to use a metaphor."

"Best ones I know are about love," Maximus said with a grin. "Love is fire."

"Love is rapture," Alessandro said, the memory of making love with Trinity instantly providing the right word.

"Love is a trap," she said, her expression tight and haunted.

"I think we'd best get a move on," Alessandro said, uncomfortable with her choice of word. Did she really feel that way about love? He dumped the dregs of his coffee on the snow. Something else had shifted in the stillness. Something unknown. It stole his attention away from his worry over Trinity and how badly she had been hurt in the past to feel that way about the wonderful experience that love could be.

Maximus gave a casual but thorough look around.

"Yes, let's see how much farther we travel before our twelve hours is up."

His brother didn't mention that the sense of something in the wind had him on high alert as well. Keeping anything that could upset Trinity from her knowing was a priority. What she would be going through in this next while was more than enough for one lifetime. If only he could protect her from the change. But since olden times, it was the way of things, and no man or beast could alter destiny. No amount of money in the world could help with it either.

As soon as they were underway, his body tensed by worry, Alessandro kept a sharp eye out for anything moving or out of place on the flat horizon. But the hours passed without incident and finally it was time to set up camp for the night.

He and Maximus quickly unpacked the sled, set up the three-person tent then saw to the feeding of vast quantities of frozen salmon to the team. He glanced at Trinity from time to time, but she seemed preoccupied, her thoughts obviously elsewhere.

He wanted to hover over her, make her feel better or come clean about what was bothering her, but he kept his distance. He wasn't like his brother Cristaldo, who tended to always be in his mate's face, for heaven's sake, picking her up like a caveman and hauling Everly to his lair the day they met! Of course, the blood moon had greatly influenced their pairing, but, still, it wasn't Alessandro's style. He wanted his mate to come freely to him, to be with him because she wanted it more than anything else on earth — not because he had money or because she felt she had no other place to turn. Being chosen was the only way it meant anything. To love and be loved in return. Was it too much to ask?

"I'll take the first watch," Alessandro said. Guarding her, keeping her from harm, was all that mattered now. This was no time for romance or worrying about the future. He needed to keep his mind directed on the immediate, staying on high alert for any whiff of danger.

"Fine. Wake me at the first inkling of anything unusual."

"I'll take a shift," Trinity spoke up, her eyes fierce with conviction.

"No! Absolutely not," Maximus said.

"I'm no hothouse flower, damn it! I signed on for a great deal of money to help acquire a valuable relic. The least I can do is pull my own weight." The skin on her face tensed with anger, her eyes darkened by emotions that Alessandro could only guess at.

"There will be no arguing about this. You stay in the tent."

"Fine, then you both can sleep outside!"

Never had he seen her angrier. Her sense of outrage seemed out of proportion with the offense. Something was going on with his mate, something that sent a streak of worry slithering coldly through his veins.

Trinity whirled around and stalked into the tent, disappearing with disapproval obvious in every line of her body.

"Well, that went well," Maximus deadpanned.

"Something's up with her."

"Do you think? She's being ravished within by hormones and changes and things out of her control. Of course something's up with her."

"No, it's more than that. She's hiding something from us." Alessandro was certain of it now. Not knowing exactly what it was so he would know how to help her, that was the hardest part. She could rant and rave at him all day, and he could take it. It was shutting him out that hurt the most. There was no clear psychic link with their mate, not yet. Just indeterminable flashes that offered no insight. Was she in contact with the one who bit her? Was that the problem? He didn't want to say it aloud. It would make the sense of fear of betrayal too real.

"She just needs a good night's sleep. We'll keep watch together. Give her space."

"Well, that's a first." Alessandro gave his brother a half smile, his interest piqued by the unexpected revelation.

"What are you going on about?" Maximus turned from scanning the horizon to look him directly in the eyes.

"I quote, *give her space*. Never thought I'd hear those words out of your mouth."

"Well, never had to figure out the minefield that is Trinity Wells before and I don't want to screw it up — all right with you?"

The last was said a bit testy. Right, his brother was not in his usual controlled head space. Then the feeling of contentment drained away in the next thought. What if Maximus was hurt badly by all this? Alessandro swallowed, not wanting to go there. *Stay in the moment.*

"You should sleep first. I got this, bro," he said.

"I'll sleep when I'm dead," Maximus snorted. "No way can I rest right now, not with everything going on."

"Yeah, I hear you."

They both settled back into their camp chairs to keep watch. They hadn't lit a fire earlier, knowing that it would give their location away. Instead, they'd cooked the steaks and baked potatoes over a camp stove fueled by smokeless propane cylinders. But staying warm was not a concern for him and his kind. Seemed some kind of anti-freeze fueled their bodies while the dark night posed no problem either with their spectacular eyesight. It was at such moments he experienced pathos for the human condition that *didn't* allow the change. And he was humbly grateful for his DNA that guaranteed it. To enter the realm that allowed him to become a wolf was a gift. Certainly, it came with challenges, but those he would bear with pride and dignity. Well, unless something or someone threatened his mate, then all bets were off. Then it was tooth and nail and death to the vanquished.

"You know they're coming for us, right?"

Alessandro nodded, deep in thought, something the emptiness of the northern landscape seemed to bring on in abundance.

"Do you think she's feeding it to them?"

"Doesn't matter. It wouldn't be her fault. You know those damn Ribelle curs and their mind-control tricks. They deserve to be kicked to the curb if they're the ones stalking her."

"I just want to get moving and find that damn chalice already!" Maximus' voice gave away the fact that he was poised on a knife's edge, ready to spring into action at the suggestion of a threat to their mate.

"We will, bro. I'm just as afraid of losing her as you are. Maybe more."

Maximus didn't ask what he meant. They both knew. The pain of losing their Forever Mate was not something they would come back from. Not as they were, but changed in ways they could not foresee. One chance at true love, and one chance only.

The long, dark night passed with the pair of them sitting back-to-back, allowing them to cover a full three-sixty sweep of the landscape. The silence between them didn't end until Trinity exited her tent hours later into the blackness of a Polar Night.

"You're up early," she observed, her eyes wary.

Alessandro didn't share that they'd spend the entire night on watch. It was what an alpha did for their mate, no more than what was expected.

"Hungry?" he asked.

"I don't want a fuss. Just a protein bar or two will suffice. I'd like to get going."

"I've made hot coffee. Soon as you're ready, we can be on our way."

She ran the tip of her tongue over her lips, not in a way to tease, but in thoughtful pose. "I need to share something will you both. And it can't wait."

Chapter Twenty

Trinity

She had their full attention, that was obvious. With two pairs of creamy brown eyes focused on her increasing tenfold the power of their alpha maleness, she almost backed down from what she had been preparing all night long to say...after Alessandro had suggested that she stay with them forever. She was so out of her depth on this journey. She had no idea what had possessed her to undertake it? But she was here now and she had to step up and do the right thing.

"I haven't been telling you everything. You know — about what's been going on with me."

"Are you in pain?" Alessandro asked.

"Yeah, but not the kind you mean." She hedged, licking her lips. She had to stop doing that. They were getting chapped from the cold.

"What kind?" Maximus asked.

"I've been getting messages in my head. From someone." She rubbed her forehead, thinking about it. It wasn't something she liked to admit to. "I think you're right about the Ribelles. They're in my head, asking for things."

"Your location, right?" Alessandro asked. He didn't look that perturbed by her admission, like he expected it. She frowned, forcing herself to go on.

"Yeah. And the worst part, I can't seem to shield my brain from them. I've tried to send them on a wild-goose chase, to think about places I've visited in detail, like historical places in Italy in particular to throw them off the scent. Even to building a wall in my mind, brick by brick, in efforts to keep them out. But I'm not certain it's working."

"The fact that you tried, that you told us about it, that's all that matters, Trinity," Alessandro said, his voice filled with such admiration and hope that she let out a huge breath of relief.

"Thanks for understanding. I admit, I wasn't expecting that."

"What were you expecting?" Maximus asked, watching her carefully. "We're scholars like you — we go the distance to discover the truth of things."

"I thought you'd be angry. I think I'm beginning to believe in what you've been telling me more and more." She paused, trying to keep her thoughts straight in her mind. "My body's changing. I've been acting out of character. I think that dog bite did something to me — infected me with a virus. I should have blood work done, figure out what's wrong. Maybe I shouldn't have come with you. I might need a transfusion or something like that? I don't know, all I know is that something's wrong."

"The artifact that we are seeking, it's supposed to help with that. We need to try that first, then if it doesn't work, get the best medical team money can buy on your case," Alessandro said. His face was troubled, as if he didn't believe a word he said about a medical team being able to help. What was it about the chalice that they had such faith in it? It was ancient, what power could it possibly have in the present?

"Okay, a day or two shouldn't make any difference, right? I'm not dying here, just confused."

A sharp look of concern from the pair. They were far more worried than she was. Her heart did a double-tap. At least she felt better for coming clean about what was going on with her.

"What, does this artifact come with instructions of usage like only drink some kind of strange concoction out of it on a full moon—like ground up bat wings and poison from a toad?" she half-joked to ease her roiling stomach.

"Not sure of what condition we'll find it in, though it made a lot of sense to bury it on the freezing tundra to preserve it. Does it have any instructions? That might be too much to hope for," Alessandro said.

"No more speculation. Let's hit the road," Maximus said, throwing the dregs of his coffee cup aside. He began packing up and Alessandro followed suit. Trinity hurried to do her fair share and when she got between them, handing off some of the kitchen items to load on the sled, a sizzling flash of electricity bore down on her, centred in her loins. She stumbled and the brothers reached for her to keep her from falling. Wedged between them, the lust only intensified. *Not this again.*

"Are you okay? What is it?" the brothers asked in tandem.

She clenched her jaw, totally incapable of answering their inquiry.

The wave passed, leaving her sweaty and more on edge than ever. She glanced at Alessandro and saw the wolf in him for the first time. His eyes had gone bright blue, his expression sharper, needful, predatory and frightening. A second glance at Maximus confirmed it.

"I—I'm all right. It passed." But it was not all right and she wasn't certain it ever would be again. The amorous thoughts had been replaced by an ominous image of wolves fighting to the death while she was helpless to do anything. Was it her destiny? The brothers' destiny? To have found each other in this harsh world only to be separated? Because, in the same way her parents had married only three days after they'd met, these two men were important to her. *More important than they should be in such a short period of time.*

"What did you see?" Alessandro asked, his eyes fading to a more natural hue. She breathed easier with the scholar back in control.

"I think things are conspiring around us. Things meant to separate us. Harm us."

The pair pulled her into a tight hug, and sandwiched between them, she felt the security of place for once in her life. To have that sense all day, every day—it was a luxury she dared not hope for. Today, that was all she could comprehend. Tomorrow would have to take care of itself.

"We will never leave you. That's our vow made under these Alaskan skies."

The words spoken in chorus by the twins touched her to the core. She let out a shuddering breath, too filled with emotion for words. She struggled for what to say in return.

"I think that's the most romantic words anyone has ever uttered in my presence." She gave them a watery smile. "I know that we're going to be tested by fire now. It's been building since we met. And I vow to stay strong, and stay true to you. And tonight, fate willing, I want us all in the same tent."

A silence greeted her promise, the darkness of the Polar Night causing a crystal-clear cocooning of them as they hovered together, gaining strength from the contact.

"Okay," Maximus said, the first one to break away. "With that to look forward to later, I'm going to be pushing as hard as I can today. Hope you're all up for it?" His voice was raw, muffled by emotion, but neither Alessandro nor Trinity made mention of it.

"I'll drive the team first today," Alessandro announced before striding over to the dogs that waited patiently to be harnessed up and set on the trail.

"No way," Maximus objected.

"Okay, let's toss for it." Alessandro reached in his pocket and drew out a coin. "Let fate decide."

When his brother won the toss, Maximus pursed his lips. "Well, I get to snuggle our mate first. No loss in that."

She treasured the sound of that word. *Mate.* Just hearing it made her feel stronger and more worthy.

With the dogs straining briefly at their leashes to break the runners free of the ice, in seconds they were underway, the frigid morning haze obscuring a landscape darkened by the perpetual lack of sunshine. *How do people endure weeks of this darkness?* Seasonal affective disorder had to be a factor for some living beyond the Artic circle. She loved the sun, finding it as necessary as breathing. No way could she ever commit to living full time in the north. She would remain a southern girl, through and through.

With Maximus' arms wrapped around her, snuggled within the layers of wool blankets, she basked for a time in the comfort provided. Then images once more began creeping into her brain, upsetting the tranquility of the early morning. Images of a terrible battle. Was it real? Or just her mind warring with itself? The discombobulation of endless nights could not be ruled out either.

"We will keep you safe," Maximus said, giving her a hard squeeze. His low-pitched voice rumbled through her, providing comfort and support, like he knew what she was seeing in her head. *Can he do that? So many questions with no answers.* If only she wasn't so confused by the changes in her body.

Sometimes she was tortured by pins and needles pricking her skin in endless waves, other times she was too horny for words. If this was the cost of changing into a wolf, as the twins suggested was happening, it sucked to high heaven. *If only I could go back in time and stay at a different motel.*

But then she wouldn't have met Maximus and Alessandro, and that experience she would never want to give up. *Always a cost. The price of existence. Suck it up, Trinity. Change is inevitable, welcomed or not.* What was it that Einstein had quoted about it? *The measure of intelligence is the ability to change. Well, dear Albert, don't think I could do much more changing than into a wolf.*

The endless miles of snow-covered terrain, the cold bringing tears to her eyes, the view only interspaced by the occasional cairn set upon the landscape... The symbolic human markers they followed gave her an uncomfortable sensation of being a character in a vampire movie, forever racing up the mountain in a carriage pulled by black horses, drawn to the beast with mesmerizing abilities and hypnotizing eyes.

If only Maximus or Alessandro could send her silent messages instead of those damn Ribelles. Would that be possible, once she went through the change? The idea of telepathy intrigued her. She'd always been open to the idea of psychic gifts, perhaps more so than the average university scholar. It surely had to aid the path of true love, in her opinion, opening channels of communication like no other.

She could only imagine letting her lovers know what felt good, what she wanted more of, without having to actually ask aloud. Though the twins didn't seem to need any prompting in that direction, ready at any opportunity to make love with her. She vowed now not to let anything else get in the way of her enjoying them. Because no matter what they said, she knew for certain that this magical, odd, infuriating time spent with the pair was not permanent.

She'd vowed years ago never to tie herself down, to live her life free of the bonds of matrimony. She'd seen too much of how her mother and father had manipulated the other. No man was ever getting the upper hand over her. But great sex, sure, she'd embrace that with all her worth.

"The Luceres can't save you. Only we can save your life. You will die if you stay with them."

The stark words focused her into a state of panic. *What the hell! Get out of my mind!*

No words followed her tirade, but doubts lingered. Were the Ribelle the ones that could save her life?

Would it come to that? *Damn it, I'm strong. I don't need anyone to save my life.* But it made the fact that she was going to undergo a transformation all that more real. The inevitable was pressing in now, driven home by the dark and doom surrounding them.

It was then that she became aware of the full moon rising over the tundra. It had crept up on her, this brightness sneaking into the night sky sending shafts of light reaching into the darkness toward them. When it crossed their path, all the air rushed out of her body. And when it touched the little bit of skin exposed on her face that the wool scarf didn't cover, it stirred her blood. It forced her attention and warmed her just before her bitten arm began to itch and throb intensely.

A suffocating sensation hit then and she nearly leapt from the sled. It was by the barest of margins she held herself in position, aided by the strong arms that circled her.

"Stop the sled!" Maximus shouted at his brother.

The dog team immediately slowed down at Alessandro's command before coming to a complete halt.

Maximus instantly threw the blankets off her and helped her off the sled. She could barely hold still as she rocked back and forth in place, her boots digging into the fallen snow, the twins hovering over her.

"Are you okay?" The worry was obvious in Maximus' tone, his haunted expression mirrored by his brother's.

"I don't know. I feel really odd. What's going to happen to me? Explain your theory to me, please. I need to understand what you're hiding from me." Her teeth were chattering from the cold and an uneasy sensation had latched on tight, making her skin feel like it was going to peel right off any second.

"This werewolf situation sucks, by the way," she added, not wanting to lose her sense of humor and perspective amongst the chaos. But losing her dignity would be the least of her worries if what the twins told her was true, that she was becoming a werewolf. Standing on the cusp of a Polar Night and a full moon rising, somehow the miracle of being turned into a wolf seemed plausible. *Just another bit of earthly magic. There are more things in Heaven and Earth, Horatio, than are dreamt of in your philosophy.* The Bard had said it best.

"We have to be completely honest with her, Maximus. You want to tell her, or should I?"

"Go ahead. We don't have much time."

"I know this is hard to hear and, believe me, it's just as hard for me to say, but a human bitten by a werewolf will become a wolf on the night of the next full moon...or die trying. The blood chalice we're seeking is supposed to save the life of any human in that condition. We have no idea how it works, or if it will work, but we're close to finding out. Really close. The inukshuk we seek is less than five miles away, if the map's correct. If you can just hang on another hour, we'll be there."

"I can. Just help me on the sled and hold on tight."

In mere seconds Maximus had her lifted back on the sleigh, his arms snugly embracing her, blankets tucked around her body. Her mind raced with the information Alessandro had shared, her pulse beating madly as they once more picked up speed, the dogs straining at their traces.

Time stood still, everything seeming in slow motion as they advanced across the never-ending snowscape. Then wolf howls suddenly drew her attention. *What was that? Are they a threat?* She peered all around, but could see nothing out of place. It was only Maximus' arms tightening around her that told her the truth. Trouble was on its way.

Finally, after she had nearly given up hope, the largest cairn she'd ever seen except in mythological tales appeared, its human shape looking like an ancient god rising up and guarding the land. Backlit by moonglow, its ghostly appearance took her away from the common era for a moment, making her wonder about the people who had erected it and the life they had lived. The study of anthropology had sometimes called her name and now it tugged even harder at her.

She sent a silent prayer to the stone man. *I want to live to learn more. Please let me live. Reveal your secrets so that I might live.*

Alessandro drew the sled to a stop a few feet from the towering figure. Maximus helped her out and the three of them advanced toward the monument.

"What are we looking for?" she asked, hugging her body with her arms in efforts to contain the discomfort of another wave of aching pain sluicing through her.

"They can't have buried it here. The ground's too frozen with permafrost. It must be located inside it somehow," Maximus observed.

The two brothers inspected the statue, circling it many times, looking for some clue.

"Do you think we need to take it apart, stone by stone? It seems a shame—it's been here for eons of time," Alessandro asked.

"Tear it down for all I care. We have to find it," Maximus said, clipping his words. He busied himself running his hands over every boulder, looking for purchase.

"It's forbidden to destroy an inukshuk. You must know that?" she said, swallowing her doubts. Perhaps a loose stone would lead the way?

"Look at this one. A heart-shaped stone that would be barely visible to the human eye," Alessandro said, excitement building in his voice, pointing out a stone near the center. "That must be important."

The pair of them began to tug at the stone, checking to see if it would lift away and leave the others intact. When it came away in their hands and the inukshuk remained standing, she drew a shaky breath.

"It's got something hidden in behind it!" Now it was Maximus' turn to become enthused by potential discovery. He reached inside the manlike structure, pulling out an ancient rusted-iron relic no larger than a shoe box. He held it with reverence, his eyes aglow with a bright blue light, now mirrored by his twin.

"Open it, bro," Alessandro urged as he replaced the stone.

The box was so badly rusted that it took precious minutes with a Leatherman tool that Maximus produced from his pocket to break the seal and lift the top off.

The three of them gathered closer together to peer inside. Maximus peeled the many layers of woven fabric away, exposing the relic for the first time in untold centuries to view.

"Such a simple-looking cup that it's hard to believe it has special powers." Trinity was the first to speak. It did indeed look ordinary, a small drinking cup that looked to be carved from whitened bone without decoration or embellishment. Certainly not a million-dollar item, to the naked eye.

"It is more precious than anything else on Earth if it can do what the legend suggests," Alessandro murmured, his expression reverent. "It may save your life, Trinity, which makes it worth all the riches this planet possesses. I would give up my fortune to see you safe. To keep you with us."

His words hit her hard, the meaning clear. If she lived through these next few hours, her life would be forever entwined with these two men, one way or the other.

A multitude of wolf howls resounded around them, much closer than before, drawing their attention from the cup. Chills raced down her spine and stirred her blood, the song of the night creatures filling her with longing. She finally understood the concept of the call of the wild.

"They're getting close. We have to start back. Now!" Maximus wrapped the cup back in its thick cloth padding and thrust the package into the pocket of his parka. Alessandro took the rusty box and hid it on the sled under the pack.

"Let's go," Maxims said, taking up the reins this time.

Fearful of what this dark day would yet bring, Trinity allowed herself to be placed back securely in the sled. Leaving the otherworldly man-like figure behind, they took off with a sickening lurch. The dogs began barking loudly, straining at their traces, as if they knew something supernatural now stalked them.

Chapter Twenty-One

Maximus

Quicker.

He urged the dogs onward, telepathing to his brother that the dogs were running at top speed. How long they could endure it was another matter. Soon they would need to rest then the truth of who or what moved against them would be known.

Then everything changed in a single beat, the sled suddenly surrounded on three sides by a pack of wolves running alongside them. The wolves were desert gray, making them seem like phantoms in the moonlight. He counted six, the sled barrelling along between them. The dogs raced faster still, their fear pushing them onward. But then they were flagging, their strength spent as the adrenaline drained from their marrow.

"Six against two, bro. We stand a chance."

"Better to die here than to lose our mate."

Maximus pulled the sled to a halt. The wolves pushed against the sled, their larger, more powerful bodies making the dogs cower in terror.

"We must change if we have a chance to win against them."

But before they could strip off their clothes, one of the wolves slipped through to the other dimension, then back as a man.

Rocco.

Naked as the day he was born. In disgust that their mate was exposed to the sight, Alessandro threw a blanket at the man, then stepped out of the sled to confront the pack alongside his brother.

"Why are you here?" Maximus demanded. A growl rumbled from deep inside his brother's chest.

"I'm here to take the female and the Lupus Sanguis Chalice."

"You have no right to be here. And if you think for one second —"

"But we do. Look around. We outnumber you three to one, Luceres. We've gone Nomad. I'm starting my own pack in the north, meaning you're subject to our laws now. And I demand my rights as pack alpha to the female bitten by a Nomad and the cup to save her life."

Rocco and five others had broken away from the House of Ribelle? This spelled trouble of major proportions as Nomads had less to lose. How to keep them from just taking what they wanted if they decided to attack all at once?

"What? You don't have the balls to fight for her. I challenge your right," Maximus said.

"I can just take what I want. Why would I need to fight?"

"Are you scared, too chicken to fight me, dog?" Maximus goaded him. The only chance they had to end this was a challenge. "Afraid you'll lose like you did to Cristaldo?"

The wolves growled at the slur on their alpha, moving in closer.

"I accept your challenge. Let's end this. Prepare to die, cur."

Maximus threw off his clothes, entering and exiting the portal in mere seconds, back from the other side as wolf, ready to fight for his mate.

"You keep her safe, brother."

His sibling acknowledged his words with a deep rumbling growl.

The other wolves backed off. Maximus and Rocco began to stalk each other, taking the measure of their opponent. Maximus was under no illusions. This would be a brutal fight. They were both alphas, at the height of their strength and power. No way could this end well for one of them. He bared his fangs, ready. No one but his twin and him would ever touch their mate.

Destroy. I will tear this bastard apart, limb by limb, before he touches one hair on her head.

He launched himself at the enemy, his claws, extended, slicing into his opponent's side, drawing first blood. But Rocco was ready, throwing his body hard against him, nearly knocking him off his feet.

Blood dripped from the cur's side, but his eyes spoke of a murderous rage, their bright blueness shining like pinpricks. Rocco struck out at him, and he ducked at the last second, sharp claws missing by scant inches.

End this.

Maximus charged the cur, knocking him off his feet, his jaws working to find purchase on the unprotected belly. Rocco scrambled out of the way, his claws scrambling against a rock trying to gain purchase. But before Rocco could regain his footing, Maximus went for his throat, jaws parted, clamping his fangs deep into hide and gristle. Rocco raked his claws over Maximus' chest, drawing second blood.

Bloodied but unbowed, Maximus slammed his body hard against the other wolf, attempting to intimidate and knock the bastard off his feet. They both went down, their bodies a blur of movement as they rolled across the snow, claws and fangs doing brutal damage as both struggled to inflict the final death blow.

Sensing his opponent weakening, Maximus pushed himself harder, the ancient beast surfacing, enraged by another male attempting to take their female. The red-hot all-encompassing fury boiled to the surface, giving him the strength of twenty men. He forced the other alpha onto his back, his teeth sinking into his belly, ready to rip and tear.

The other wolves began to howl, a song of fear that their alpha would die this day. Maximus heard the din through his blood rage. Did he really want his mate to see him kill another? It took all he had, but he stopped himself just short of the final strike, waiting for the other wolf to submit.

Rocco lay still, belly exposed. He had surrendered.

Maximus stepped back, blood dripping from his muzzle, his legs planted wide in victory.

The pack surrounded their alpha, encouraging him to get back up. Rocco scrambled to his feet now that the threat had back off, growling and baring his teeth once more.

"I have enough wolves to take you down, Luceres." The cur had the audacity to send the message into his mind.

Maximus spun in anger, confronting his opponent once more. *"You know the rules. You lost the challenge. Now you must concede."*

Rocco shook his massive head, blood dripping onto the white snow in darkened patches from the wounds to his belly. *"You have no one to call. We will end this here, take the female."*

Alessandro joined him, standing tall at his side. If they died this day, they died together. His one regret was not having more time with their mate, showing her how good life could be sharing hers with the two of them. If only they had claimed and marked her this wouldn't be happening. But to do so could have threatened her health, and that he would not do.

"Word of this betrayal to all we hold dear will eventually spread. Are you certain you want to breach an ancient rule? My pack will come after you. You must that know that."

"Bring it on, mutt. Try to find us in this vast landscape. We will have the female and the chalice. Nothing else matters."

The brothers sprang in tandem at the alpha to take him down first. With him dead, the others might step down. But before they could finish him off, the Rocco pack threw themselves into the fray, teeth gnashing and claws fully extended, prepared to do maximum damage to the brothers.

It was a day he would not have chosen to die, but if the fates wanted it, then he and his brother would met in the afterlife, for he knew it existed. He'd seen it and was unafraid of death because of it, but had just the single, driving worry of leaving their mate alone to fend for herself. *Trinity, forgive me, if I don't live out this day. We will wait for you on the other side.*

Loud howls erupted around them, drawing the attention of the other wolves. When Maximus looked around to see what was happening, Rocco took the opportunity to slice deep into his throat with sharp claws. He staggered back from the blow, barely keeping his feet. Blood poured onto the snow-covered ground from the massive wound, staining it dark. Core blood, darkest of all.

Suddenly, the fighting wolves were surrounded by a multitude of white wolves, far exceeding a dozen or more. So many that Rocco's pack stopped dead in their tracks, their fear apparent by the offensive odor of their unwashed bodies.

"You are not welcome in the north, curs. Your lack of honor and courage brands you traitors. Go and never come back. Stay and die. Choose." The telepathic voice of the alpha male boomed and echoed against the night sky.

The gray wolves slunk off, their tails low, vanishing over the horizon. Rocco sent out one last dagger-fueled message — *"It's not over yet, cur"* — before he, too, turned and left the vicinity.

Maximus took a deep breath, the blood beginning to slow from his nearly mortal wound, giving him hope. He was weak, but he would live, he decided fiercely. He wanted a life with Trinity and Alessandro.

He glanced at the huge alpha standing before him. Was this massive white wolf Tikaani? He wasn't certain, but he suspected it was the truth.

"Thank you for coming to our aid."

"You are welcome, Luceres, to come onto our land in the future. To share food and drink with us. We would escort you back to town, if you wish it?"

"No. They won't be back now. You've broken their spirit. I thank you for coming to our aid this day. It will not be forgotten. Call us when you have need and we will come. My brother and I, and others of the Luceres pack."

"Your mate, she is unwell?"

His asking drew Maximus' attention to the sled. *"Yes, we are going to try to heal her."*

"Good. We will stay and guard the perimeter until all is well."

Maximus nodded his head with reverence for the support. The pack of white wolves turned and left, leaving them with much-needed privacy.

Chapter Twenty-Two

Alessandro

"You're badly hurt. You need to rest, brother. You'll heal faster as a wolf." Alessandro slipped through the portal and back, redressing quickly.

"No time. We must figure out how the chalice works."

He watched Maximus push himself to enter the next dimension, his worry intensified by the sight of his brother's wounds, blood still dripping and staining the ruff of fur on his chest. When Maximus faltered, Alessandro rushed to stop him.

"Stay as you are. I'll see to Trinity."

Maximus growled, his displeasure obvious.

Alessandro hurried to check on Trinity, leaving his brother to lick his wounds and begin the healing process. She lay slumped in the sled, her eyes closed. He came closer and gently touched her cold, pale cheek.

"Are you all right?" he asked, keeping his voice low and reassuring.

She opened her eyes, blinking a few times, looking confused. Then she recognized him and offered a weak smile. "Alessandro, I'm not feeling very well." Her voice was tinged with worry.

"You're going to be fine, beautiful." If only he believed it.

"Are you hurt? Is Maximus...all right? I heard so much fighting...I thought the worst."

"Don't speak. Save your energy, sweetheart. We're going to make your well. Just be patient."

"Where is...Maximus? I need to see that he's...okay."

Alessandro heard the wolf whine at his back and knew that his brother was in terrible pain. Not just physical, but worse, emotional anguish at not being able to be there for their mate in her most desperate time of need.

"He's just healing for a few minutes. We Luceres wolves are strong, but we need a tittle while to heal after such a big battle."

"Was he hurt?" Trinity struggled to sit up, but it was obvious her body was now too weak to support itself.

"He'll be fine." His reassurance that rang a bit false even to his ears, and he hoped she wouldn't pick up on it.

She licked her lips.

"Are you thirsty?"

"A bit."

He assisted her to drink a few sips of water, then laid her back in the brace of blankets. *Time to deal with the chalice.* Surely there had to be a clue as to its use? Picking up Maximus' parka, he retrieved the cup from the pocket. Unwrapping it, he inspected it closely. Nothing stood out on its smooth, carved surface. The size of a teacup, its insides were darker as if some substance had stained it eons ago. *Could it be blood? Blood and bone. The essentials of life lived in our DNA.* An idea surfaced. Perhaps adding pure water to the cup would activate something? But how long to leave it before having Trinity drink from it?

Picking up a bottle of water, he unscrewed the lid and poured a few ounces into the cup, then set it aside, propped carefully to keep the water from spilling.

He turned to check on his brother, relieved to see him lying prone on the ground resting, though Alessandro was worried about his labored breathing. *Soon he should have his strength back*, he reassured himself. In the meantime, he decided to set up camp. *No point in moving on until the final outcome.* What that would be was not something he could contemplate right now. No, he needed to keep his wits about him, for all three of them.

Within a few minutes, he had unloaded the tent and supplies, and was feeding the dogs and setting about preparing food. Though normally famished after a fight, he found his appetite was nearly nonexistent, but it gave his hands something to do while he waited.

"Give me some of that steak, bro. It will help."

Maximus got to his feet, his actions stiff as he worked his limbs. It was then that Alessandro realized it was not just a wound to his brother's throat, but multiple bite wounds all over his body. *Those damn Ribelles!* Alessandro wanted revenge for their betrayal in the worst way, but he kept his emotions under wraps. No time or energy for what could wait.

He slipped the largest steak off the propane burner and set it in front of his brother, then watched as he gulped it down. Yes, Alessandro needed to eat as well. Maximus was right, it was no time to be weak. He forced himself to eat some of the steak, choking it down with gulps of water.

"*More steak?*"

Maximus ignored Alessandro's question, asking instead, "*How is our mate?*"

"*She's weak, but all right at the moment.*"

The food did the trick and within a few seconds, his brother was through the wormhole-like portal and back, the white gleam of sparking light around him the only sign of entrance and exit. Though pale, he looked better, even smeared with blood as he was.

Alessandro handed his brother a large bottle of water which he used to clean himself. After drying off, he re-dressed.

"Any clues to how the chalice works?" Maximus asked.

Alessandro explained his idea.

"Good. How long should we wait?"

"I don't know. Maybe it's time to try?"

"Yes, I'm all for it."

The twins hovered over Trinity, Maximus propping her up and Alessandro offering her a few sips from the precious cup.

When she had downed as much as she was able, they stood back to watch. Minutes passed, but still she looked pale and weak, unable even to open her eyes now.

Alessandro leaned down and kissed her lips as gently as if he were touching the wings of a butterfly. "Come back to us, beautiful. I need you. We need you."

Maximus lightly stroked her forehead, his eyes softened by worry and love.

"Stay with us, *tesoro*. We love you."

She stirred at his words, but seemed unable to speak.

"It's not working. What should we do?"

"Was it just water in the cup?" Maximus asked, his forehead creased by a frown.

"Yes, there appeared to be blood residue or some dark substance in the cup, and I thought that maybe mixing it with water would do something to release and infuse the water."

"The cup had blood in it? That's it! The transformation requires blood." Maximus' expression became intensified, his eyes shining bright blue. His wolf was also convinced.

"Yes, that's worth a try, brother," Alessandro agreed, his mind busy considering the logistics.

"Get a weapon and we'll get on with it."

Alessandro stopped himself from worrying about the blood loss than his brother had already experienced and, instead, concentrated on grabbing a wicked-looking hunting knife from the pack.

"I'll give the blood. You've already lost too much." Before his brother could object, he stood back and sliced across the palm of his hand, then began squeezing the blood into the mouth of the cup.

"How much will she need do you think?"

"Give it a good trial. Don't stint on it," Maximus said.

"Do you think we'll be able to get her to drink it?" Alessandro watched the blood drip slow down enough before he grabbed a rag to tie around his hand to stanch the flow.

"She will. She wants to live."

Alessandro held the cup to her lips while his brother bore her upright once more. When she began to gag, he stopped.

"Did she take any?" Maximus asked, his worry obvious.

"Some."

There was nothing to do but wait, but to wait was intolerable. Alessandro wanted to be doing something, *anything*, to help his mate recover. Not knowing what would work and what would not work was the hardest part. Every fiber of his being screamed for answers as he struggled not to show how upset he was.

"Is she any better?"

Alessandro leaned down and placed two fingers over her carotid artery. "Her pulse is weaker, thready. I don't think it's working. Why not?" Fear struck him harder, making his throat constrict, forcing him to work harder at taking a full breath.

"Think of the legend. What would make sense, knowing our beginnings?"

"The twin brothers, Remus and Romulus. Both nourished and raised by the she-wolf. Twins. Maybe that's it?"

"Both our blood? Mixed together? Can't hurt. Let's try it."

Alessandro reluctantly cut the palm of his brother's hand, uncomfortable with him losing even more blood. But what was there to do but to play out the hand they were dealt?

"We should say something."

"You go ahead. I'm too drained to come up with anything," Maximus admitted, his complexion paler than his brother had ever seen it.

Alessandro bowed his head, reciting the words that freely came to him. "We honor the first wolf and ask her help in aiding our mate to return to full health — to accept the challenge to become a she-wolf."

He then placed the chalice to Trinity's lips, urging her to take a sip. She valiantly took a few drops, then her head lolled back, her strength seeming totally gone.

"My God, we're losing her!" The stark words cut the very legs out from under him. He slumped onto the sled, holding on to his mate with all his might. Maximus joined them, sandwiching her body between them, adding his warmth. The moon shone brighter and the night colder as they lay entwined in the stillness. The whole world stopped.

The hours passed, but still their mate lay still as death. There would be no sunrise today, echoing the demise of his mortal soul, no doubt. For how could they go on, knowing they would never pass this way again? Never have the chance to be with their chosen mate? For there was only one destined for them, and she lay dying between them.

A series of wolf howls woke him from his stupor. He was afraid to check on Trinity, lying so quietly bathed by the surreal light of the brightest moon he'd experienced, a luminousness that spoke across the ages. It made him want to weep. The three of them should be running across this tundra, capturing the essence of what it meant to be a wolf, the amazing power and gifts it brought, not frozen in the moment, with no rush of life surging through their systems. *So bloody unfair.* Everything had been within their grasp, and now, nothing but dust remained.

Even now she could be gone, traveled to the other side alone, unable to be with them until they too crossed, many, many decades from now.

How could he go on? Tears stung his eyes and ran down his cheeks. For the first time, he felt no shame at being overcome with emotion. The loss was unthinkable. More than he could bear.

Chapter Twenty-Three

Trinity

Trinity stirred, her arms instinctively reaching out for the brothers hovering nearby. When she opened her eyes, their mirrored expressions spoke of their recent ordeal, their eyes haunted by a hunger that tugged at her. She instinctively wanted to reassure them and pushed herself to show them she was fine, gifting them a hard-won smile.

"I'm feeling much better. What did you guys do? Last thing I remember, you were in a huge fight. Are you okay? I can't thank you enough for looking out for me. For not letting those animals take me."

"Of course, that's what mates do for each other," Maximus said, tucking a strand of hair behind her ear with extreme tenderness. *Did his fingers tremble?*

She remembered then what she'd seen before everything had faded to black. The strange refractions of light, almost a shimmering, that had made the air around the twins become suddenly visible, with prism rays of sky blue and white shooting outward. A human-sized breach, like a portal that glimmered, revealing a glimpse into another dimension right next to their own.

Scientists talked of eleven dimensions, a fact that boggled her mind, but what had happened next had totally blown her away and she knew she would never, ever see the world the same again. For in a blink of an eye, they had disappeared, only for something else to appear in their places. Something that should not have been there. Two giant wolves, gray fur with bright blue eyes. Then the horrific fight that she refused to think about now, instead focusing on the positive.

"I think I can see creatures moving on the moon, my vision is that darn sharp." She followed her comment with a sigh, suddenly filled to the brim with happiness that she was still alive. And what she had seen on the other side—*well, no talking about that either yet. Too overwhelming.*

"Trinity, you're okay!" Alessandro said, squeezing her so hard she could barely breathe. "I thought we'd lost you."

"Whoa, not so tight," she squealed.

"We have so much to teach you. So many wonderful new experiences for all of us to enjoy," Maximus said, his voice strong. He and his brother shared a look and she briefly wondered how bad it had been for them. They'd only known one another for such a short period of time, and yet, in some way, it was like they'd always been together. She'd like to stay friends with the pair, if they wanted it. Being the three musketeers had such a lovely ring to it.

"First thing I need is something to eat. I'm starved."

"Of course." Alessandro jumped from the sled and got busy dealing with the camp stove and their cooler of stashed food.

Maximus remained, and, reaching over and caressing her face between his two large hands, he stared right into her eyes with the most intense expression. "We thought we'd lost you. And yet here you are, back with us. It means so much to both of us. You have no idea." And with that he kissed her on the lips with such gentleness and reverence that she could do nothing but stare back at him with wonder. Where had that big bad macho alpha billionaire who had wanted to take her down for working his casino over with her card-counting gone?

It was like he heard her thoughts when he went on, "There is no money in the universe that can equal being with the one you love."

"Excuse me, but how is that even possible, loving me? You don't know me. I haven't always been a good person. I've lied and schemed for my family."

"You have a good soul. It shines through in your eyes and in your actions. I'm certain it's one of the reasons why we could save you."

This was not the time to restate her unchanged position on love. They had just been through an incredibly emotional ordeal. Later, when things calmed down, she'd remind them. "The chalice worked? How? What did you do?"

Excitement filled her as the full impact of what it meant for their kind filled her mind with amazement, as amazing as realizing she *had* a new kind. Now there would be more destined mates able to be with their chosen when they survived the change. While she had been out of reach of her mates, she'd been to a place that had shown her possibilities. This chalice could be a really good thing in the right hands. Used for good, humankind would be so much stronger with the extra powers of the wolf fused with their DNA, like it had once been eons ago.

"It did. It took the combined strength of both Alessandro's and my blood to activate it. Then it was the longest wait in the world to find out if it would work, but yes, the results are in. You survived the full moon. Today will be a day of learning how it works. We'll walk you through it. After what you just survived, this will be the easy part."

"Blood! But you had already lost so much during that horrible battle." The thought squeezed the breath from her lungs.

"There is nothing I wouldn't give up for you, *tesoro*. That's how it works in our world. Once you find your mate, everything is about making sure they are well and stay safe. That *all* their needs are met."

A certain gleam in his eyes told the full story.

"One step at a time," she protested even though the look had kick-started something else in her. Something deeper and wilder…and far more exciting.

"Your food is ready," Alessandro called out.

The fragrance of mingling scents made her throw off the load of blankets and leap out of the sled. *One urgent need at a time*, she reminded herself.

"Is that bacon I smell?" she asked, her mouth watering like crazy. She sidled up to Alessandro and nabbed a piece of bacon right out of the frypan.

"Yummy," she said over a crispy, succulent mouthful of heavenly goodness.

"Easy to make you happy," he said, his eyes filled with amusement, a much better look than the strain that had filled them for the past days.

The day without sunshine didn't bother her now. She was alive and she was going to enjoy herself.

They ate in silence, consuming every last morsel of food that Alessandro had generously prepared, then breaking out the protein bars for extra nourishment.

"I'm stuffed," she said finally, pushing herself to her feet. "I need to work off some of this food."

"Ah, the training begins," Alessandro said, a wide grin on his handsome mug. Even out in the wilderness without benefit of the usual grooming aids, he looked incredibly handsome. Both he and Maximus near took her breath away every time she glanced at them. Slightly messy hair enhanced their ruggedness, the slight scruff of not shaving for a couple of days just adding to their alure. She wondered how it would feel scraping against her tender skin. She forced her thoughts away from the lust and instead concentrated on discovering her inner wolf.

"What do I do first?" she asked.

The pair glanced toward each other with a nod, speculation high in their creamy brown eyes.

"Right!" She knew exactly what to do. She began to strip her clothes off, wondering if she needed her head examined for doing the activity in the freezing cold. Were those snowflakes or ice crystals drifting to the ground? "Yikes, it's cold! Maybe I'd better leave something on?"

"Not if you want to keep it, you don't. Though cells brimming with life pass through to the other side, dead inert things like clothes do not. First thing to remember," Alessandro lectured, like the true academic he was. Of course, it wasn't just the academic in him that watched her so intently though those glittering brown eyes. It was also the lustful man she'd already been to bed with once.

"Where am I going anyway, you know, for this change?"

"When you enter this parallel existence for the change, you shift from pure energy into a new form at the quantum level. And as you may know from studying physics, energy cannot be destroyed, only altered. It's like a frequency. You'll see a sort of 'shimmering' during the shift. It's an all-spectrum-light-energy. Not painful, and you might just lose yourself for a few seconds as your energy shifted from the human form to the wolf form. The wolf then shimmers into existence. And vice versa."

"That's some explanation." She took a deep breath, pursing her lips, enjoying the new normalcy of being healthy and sparing with them.

"The moon will trigger and power your first time. After that, you should be able to call it on at will. So, just relax and see yourself as wolf. Allow the change. Want and embrace your inner wolf," Maximus said, his expression intent with passion for teaching her what she needed to know.

"I can do that. Here goes." She had never wanted anything more in her life. The thought of the power of being a she-wolf stirred her imagination like no other idea ever had. To be a scholar and to discover such things? She would learn and do things that few humans had access to. How lucky was that?

Mid-thought, she entered another realm, a parallel existence, invisible from Earth until now, and her body underwent the change. On the other side, through the shimmering portal, the sensation deepened until all her cells had transformed, aligned in a new form. Not truly painful, but an odd feeling of discomfort and strangeness.

Then she was back in the present almost instantaneously, queasy from the shattering journey, only now in wolf form. Interestingly, the world had mutated to an array of colors unknown to the human eye, blacks and browns and grays with subtle shadings that her brain quickly converted to what her human side saw — blues and greens, yellows and reds. Amazing.

She breathed in deeply, her olfactory nerves sharpened by the cold, dry air of the Artic night with the tantalizing full moon still present. The scents of the food they'd just consumed, the odor of the dog pack, but best of all, the delicious fragrance of her twin wolves had heightened to a medley of awesomeness. Ah, but it was good to be she-wolf.

"How does it feel?"

"Indescribable. Fantastic. Unimaginable. It's beyond amazing." The words poured into her mind, transferred over to the twins in a flash. There was a difference in her own inner thoughts and those she projected, easy enough to manage. She hadn't expected that, more certain that an invasion of privacy might be something she'd have to wrestle with.

"Your chest has a huge snow-white star on it. I've never seen anything like that before." Alessandro shook his massive head in surprise.

"Just proves how special she is."

She glanced down at her chest and got a glimpse of the star-shaped fur. *Nice.*

"Ready to run?"

She didn't need to be asked twice. She took a test leap on four brand new limbs and found her sea legs immediately, racing across the tundra in huge bounds, wanting to throw off all the chains that bound her to her ordinary existence. *That's the point, right, to channel the drive and energy of the pack into a glorious rush of pure freedom?* Never again would she be made to feel lesser than by the world at large. She had the power. The new birthright to do as she damned well pleased.

Sure, she'd still help her family, but she would do it more on her own terms now. Set them straight that she wasn't their only meal ticket. That they needed to step up and be a team together, not expect her to do all the heavy lifting. It was like blinders had been narrowing her vision for years, and now that they were off, she saw things far more clearly.

"What do you think, love, is it all you imagined it to be?" Alessandro asked, running on one side of her while his brother escorted her on the other.

There was that uncomfortable word again. *Love.* They must be using it as a pet name, right? She would never mislead them. For all they'd been through, she could never be tied down. But for the first time her vow brought a slight twinge of regret. *No, stay strong, Trinity. You have you whole life ahead of you. Don't tie yourself down before it's even begun.*

"There are things we haven't shared with you yet. Things that will need to be done to keep you safe," Maximus said.

"What things? Tell me."

"The marking and claiming ceremony."

"What the hell is that?" She didn't like the sound of that.

"It's for your own protection. When a Luceres, or any wolf for that matter, takes a mate, they mark the female with a bite that leaves their scent behind to warn off other males."

"What? That's crazy talk. What if the woman says no?"

"Then it can't be done, but it leaves her vulnerable to attack from other Nomad males. Like Rocco and his new pack. We want to protect you from them. Claim you as our own.

We three were meant to be. Surely you feel it too?" Alessandro sounded surprised by her reluctance.

"Both of you?" She was filled with confusion, though a shiver of excitement ran through her at the thought of having two such virile males wanting her for their own. When this run was completed, she had big ideas of what she wanted to do next. But *none* of it included marking and claiming.

"No. I can't allow that. I've vowed never to be controlled by a man, let alone two of them." And with those words, she charged ahead of them, racing with the wind at her back.

The twins remained silent for the rest of her journey, only nudging her with their powerful bodies when they came upon a member of the group of wolves that had fought alongside them earlier. She showed her appreciation for the support of the other pack by offering a chuff of acknowledgment. It was her first greeting and it was returned. Yes, it was great to be wolf.

Back at the tent, the site of her rebirth, the three of them shifted back to human. When the pair of warrior males revealed their nakedness, she could only stare in wonder. *Such fine alpha males in their prime.* Muscles sculptured and rippling, cocks heavy and thick between strong thighs. *Oh. My. Goddess.* Her mouth watered, and not for food. She wanted to sink her teeth into all that glorious man flesh and taste the raw power.

"Now that I've eaten, discovered the joys of being a running wolf, maybe it's time to appreciate another of our earthy desires?" She stood, hands on hips, daring the two to join her in some lustful winter games. Just the touch of the chilled air on her bare skin made her body come alive, her breasts swell with anticipation. The look of pure intensity from the two men made her

feel like the most desired woman on the planet. *Ever.*
Each glance seared her skin, causing goosebumps to
erupt that had nothing to do with the cold.

Her skin had never been hotter, more sensitive.
Surely the snow under her feet should be melting like a
summer glacier from the heat simmering through her
veins and arteries?

Chapter Twenty-Four

Trinity

It took little invitation. A rush forward by the pair of brothers and she was embraced between them, Maximus' lips on hers, hungry and searching. The simple surrender to what awaited focused her mind. Her body softened, preparing to be fucked.

And when Alessandro came up behind her, placing his hands around her to grasp her breasts as if weighing their fullness, she let loose a moan. His fingers tugging at her nipples caused a gush of wetness to flow from her already swollen cunt. She wanted to be turned inside out by the stunning pair of alphas, to experience everything her new life and body had to offer. Never has she felt more invincible, more desired.

Low growls erupted from the back of the men's throats as they both tasted her skin. She had to remind herself to breathe, to overcome her impatience to get on with it, to allow them to proceed at their own pace. When Alessandro nipped at her collarbone, she shivered in anticipation. This was something she'd waited her whole life for, a moment just for her, her inner fantasy world come bursting to life. Later, there might be regrets, but also awesome memories to keep her warm all the days of her life.

"Let's head to the tent," Maximus said, his voice so low and growly it tidal-waved through her entire system, leaving hot licks of desire in its path.

On the blow-up mattress, the two men lay on either side of her, stretched out in long lines of muscle and sinew that appeared as ancient as a pair of medieval warlords. Maximus reached out, took Alessandro's hand and pressed it to her leg, moving it higher and higher and higher, lingering at the crease between her pussy and her thigh.

He did it so slowly she thought she might perish before the tangle of warm, blunt fingertips touched her quivering flesh. She grasped for breath, spreading her legs farther in an acute frenzy to be touched and fucked.

"What do you want the most, *tesoro*?" Maximus asked. "We'll give you everything and anything you desire."

"*I want to be finger-fucked, licked within an inch of my life then fucked by both of your cocks until I can't tell which way is up.*" Who was this siren who knew exactly what she wanted?

"Speak the words spoken aloud. That's far sexier," Alessandro urged.

"I'm wet for both of you. Now, please, do I have to beg you, to do what you want with me?"

"We want all of you, Trinity. Are you willing to go that far? Give us everything?" Alessandro teased her with his fingers, softly rubbing the outside of her vulva, tracing her lips over and over, driving her to distraction. *Goddess, yes.*

"Whatever you want! Just fuck me already!" She had one last moment of sanity and thought to add, "My hard limit is the claiming. And marking. But other than that, all bets are off. I'm no virgin." She was more than certain she could handle both of them. No sex position had escaped her experimenting.

Two of his fingers slid deep inside her as a different hand also pushed inside. She lifted her hips off the bed at the exquisite sensation of both men stretching her. It was dirty, it was liberating and it made her come close to losing her damn mind.

"Just relax, and we can make you ours, take you to the supreme heights of carnal pleasure," Maximus near purred. He slid his lips slid down her neck, sucking and nipping as he worked his way to her breasts. Drawing a nipple into his mouth, he pulled long and tight until her cunt once more gushed with wetness.

"You are soaking for us," Alessandro said, using his fingers to stroke against the walls of her pussy, dipping in and out and making her want more, so much more.

"Oh, yes!" she moaned. Behind her and in front of her, two men caressed her, kissed her, taking all sorts of wonderful liberties.

She reached out for Maximus' cock, stroking his balls and probing the sensitive skin of his perineum. "You like?"

"I want to dine on that sweet pussy of yours far more. This first time together — all three of — it's all about you. It's your party."

He lifted her legs wide and knelt between them. She let loose a half-scream when he used his talented mouth to capture her cunt, applying his thick, strong tongue to lick the length of her sensitive folds, swiping right through her. He found her clit and rolled it between his lips, sucking, balancing her precariously on the threshold of an orgasm. Her whole body quivered with the need for release, more urgent by the second.

"Don't stop. Please, please keep going, I'm almost there." The Luceres men knew how to touch a woman. Everything was larger than life, one man attending to her throbbing oh-so-needy pussy, the other thrumming her breasts and nipples to the point where she squealed again from the intensity of overwhelming attention. When Alessandro used his teeth to graze her shoulder, she shivered in delight, the forbidden thought of claiming entering her brain. No, she didn't want that. *Right?* To be the woman this pair of sex machines brought to orgasm every night of their lives...

"I'm going to fuck you now, make you come on my cock."

He placed her legs over his shoulders and slid his thick cock through her swollen flesh, in and out, the rhythm hard and fast. Her body shook with each push and her muscles rippled around his shaft, milking him, drawing him in tighter.

Alessandro used his fingers to slip down to where the two of them were joined, where she was spread wide open. He circled the pulsing connection of cunt and cock, timing each entry between his brother's thrusts. Taking moisture onto his fingers, he used its slipperiness to push against her sensitive anus, securing a finger easily inside.

Her entire body was on fire and open to whatever he chose to do to her. It was her gift to them for saving her life, and a forbidden gift to herself for all that she had been through and endured these past few days. The pure naughtiness of his touching her where his brother fucked her sent her into overdrive, her mind spun out of control. She howled her pleasure, her need. Alessandro pushed two more fingers inside her, stretching her, before thrusting the thick head of his cock against her ass.

Between Maximus' full strokes, Alessandro thrust inside her. *Too tight.* She had to keep herself from clenching. Then as she relaxed, adjusted to the invasion, the pair worked in tandem, one cock always buried balls-deep while the other was on the upstroke. It was pure fucking heaven. A bliss she could only have imagined. It consumed her, turned her inside out, stretched her beyond what she believed possible and she relished every amazing second of it.

"Yes, that's it. Take it all, baby. We've been waiting our whole lives for you. To fuck you like you've never been fucked before. To take you places you've never been, never knew existed," Alessandro said.

A wave of lust rose from somewhere deep inside, pushing her thoughts out beyond the borders of her normal existence. They were flying, the three of them, connected on a primal level that made the sex only part of the equation. Each dual thrust within her body was hot as hades, but nothing compared to the fire lit inside her soul.

She burned to cinders in their grasp. Trinity reached out to them from another place in time, like spirits rushing across centuries, and she welcomed it even while she felt her old self incinerate. A part of herself she hadn't realized was missing reconnected now, made her whole again. She had joined her body and spirit to the two men driving themselves so deep inside her that she had no idea where they ended and she began. And it was right and true. And almost too much to bear.

She was mute, too filled with wonder to speak. *"What is this? How can this be happening to me?"*

"We feel it too. It's the quickening. The three of us becoming one. Fate has decreed us reunited and nothing will tear us apart except death. And even then, we will find you again. We will always be each other's everything. A trio against the world. Meant to be. Chosen."

Reunited? That a single word could be such a bombshell!

"Don't you feel it? You have made us whole. We searched the entire world over for you. Then you came to us, searching for what we searched for and were desperate to find, and you helped us find it in the nick of time."

The intensity built to a fever-pitch, sweat dripping and juices mingling into an intoxicating miasma. She lost herself entirely to the waves of orgasm as they grew ever stronger, driving her body to complete release, opening and stretching her to the very limits of endurance.

She embraced it, sought it and finally succumbed to its living magic. Lust and love among the stars. She'd been to the farthest reaches of the universe and back, a wholly changed new being far beyond wolf. How could she ever leave them, knowing what she knew? But it scared her, this new intensity. How could such a thing work, last? It seemed impossible to comprehend.

When the last pleasurable tremor eased and the three of them lay still, a tangle of impossible-to-move limbs, she fell into a deep sleep, held by two incredible men.

Chapter Twenty-Five

Maximus

Maximus woke a few hours later, his mind and body completely relaxed for the first time in distant memory. He gazed at his brother and Trinity, hardly believing that their search for their new mate was finally over. That in the world of nearly seven billion inhabitants, they had found her. *Again.* He knew deep in his bones that the three of them had been together before, in multiple times and places. Flashes of that life had come alive while the three of them had been so intimately intertwined. Images of the three of them in ancient Rome by the river Tiber. The eternal city had been their first home, long before the coming to the new land during a gold rush and a fresh beginning for their bloodline.

He slipped away from the pair. The first thing he wanted to do when they got back to the inn was to have a long, hot shower. He left the tent and washed up, pulling on warm clothing, checking on the dog team foremost in his mind. The day was as dark as the night before when he stepped outside, something brand-new to his existence, something he thought he'd never get used to. *Or want to for that matter. Time to go home to Vegas. Bring our mate into the fold and start a new life. A better life.*

The dogs lumbered to their feet to greet him, their tongues lolling out with interest as he approached. Though it wasn't the normal case to feed them in the early morning, he felt the urge to fortify them before the hard journey that awaited them. He gave each a rasher of frozen salmon that was quickly consumed.

He ran his hands over the lead dog's thick fur, enjoying the sensation of the rough texture under his fingers. All the dogs were exceedingly healthy, a credit to the person or persons who had raised and trained them. Though excited to start back, to rejoin civilization, he let Alessandro and Trinity sleep their fill. The day ahead would be arduous without starting it exhausted. And their mate had to be tired after the night the three of them had shared. The most amazing night of their lives, bar none.

His cock stirred with the memory, ready for round two. His mind seared with the image of using his knot to fulfil her, as soon as she went into heat again. And judging by her scent, that could be any moment. *Then the final ceremony of claiming and marking.* So many good things awaited them and he was bursting to begin this new journey.

A slight noise drew his attention and he glanced over to see his brother exiting the tent.

"Morning. Where's the coffee and food?" Alessandro looked around in disappointment.

"I left it until you got up, lazybones. You do a better job of it anyway," Maximus said with a cocky grin.

"Lazy? Is that the best you got? Considering how you've left all the meal prep to me?" His brother gave him a look, one eyebrow arched. But he quickly opened the stove top, lit the burner and got down to the business of preparing a hearty breakfast.

"How's our *tesoro*?" Maximus asked.

"Beautiful and just getting up. She'll be out in a moment. Not sure she's a morning person though. She seemed a bit out of it." Alessandro frowned.

"She's been through a lot, more than most people could bear. Give her some space and she'll be fine."

"Since when did you become a relationship coach?" Alessandro shot back. He was right, normally that would be his brother's domain.

"We'll keep her so busy fucking us that she'll have no time for regrets." The thought pleased him, but apparently not their mate when she suddenly emerged from the tent and glared at him.

She stomped over to a camp chair and sat.

Alessandro immediately handed her a bottle of water and a protein bar. "Here you go, beautiful lady. This will tide you over. Breakfast will be ready soon."

"Thanks." She set to work on the high-calorie protein bar, washing it down with gulps of water.

"Better?"

She nodded, her expression guarded, like she had a secret she didn't want to share. Maximus' stomach twisted in his worry that they had missed something. Something important.

"Everything okay, *tesoro*?" he asked.

"Mmm."

A series of howls in the distance riveted all their attention onto the horizon. Rocco and his pack of curs, or their new allies from town?

Breakfast turned into a quick affair with no time to question their mate further, followed by a hurried dismantling of the tent and repacking.

The race across the tundra worked to clear his mind, the dogs straining at their traces a powerful lesson in endurance. He had insisted on driving the sled, needing the time. Alessandro would be more equipped to deal with their mate anyway. She was not quite herself this morning, that was obvious, barely speaking two words while they packed up and safely tucked her aboard.

But her scent, oh her scent, was changing. It was so enticing that it was all he could do not to push her to the ground and fuck her silly. *Find out what the problem is.* Another reason he'd chosen to handle the team today — he was going out of his mind at the knowledge that she was going into heat. The sooner he got them back to the inn, the better.

Chapter Twenty-Six

Trinity

Uncomfortable didn't begin to cover the uneasy sensations nearly overtaking all her common sense. After a luxurious night of three-way sex, she wanted more. Lots and lots more. Her body had apparently woken up last night, fighting to be the one in charge. It was only by the slimmest margins that she was holding on to her dignity and not throwing herself at the two virile men. And oh, they were virile. No mistaking that. They knew exactly what would please her, take her to the highest levels of sensual pleasure. *Bloody sex machines*. They had no business being billionaires as well. *Some people get all the damn luck*. She rubbed at her forehead with a thickly mittened hand, her brain roiling with the events of the past twenty-four hours.

What did they want with her? She was a nobody. A woman with excess baggage, though she was learning how to deal with that, especially when her wolf side spoke up. But she was definitely a woman who didn't want to be tied down. But how on earth was she going to walk away from them? They swore she was the one for them. The things she'd experienced, the things revealed during their lovemaking, all confused the hell out of her.

She'd never wanted to be a woman too weak to make up her own mind. *Never mind give control to the male of the species.* She'd always kept herself safe by living alone, walking away before things got messy. And now two men wanted to share her life? It didn't make sense to her. She wanted to run from them, from the wild desires they so effortlessly brought to the surface, and yet underneath her confusion, she desperately wanted to stay. Which was the right course of action? Maybe it came down to which decision would hurt less? *Run away now, put up with the intense pain that would surely follow, or wait and see how things go?*

The closer the sled traveled toward the northern outpost, the more certain she became that leaving the twins was not an option. The pain would be unimaginable. But neither was she going to put up with being marked and claimed. Instead, why not just ride the most incredible wave of her life? Because from what they had already experienced as a trio, it was going to be the biggest, baddest tsunami event in the history of ménages. And she was right in the middle of it.

The sled came to a sudden halt.

"What's up?" she asked, turning and checking in with Alessandro snuggled in behind her.

"If we want to get home tonight, we should remove all the gear and supplies we can, then shift to wolf form to give the team a break," Alessandro explained.

"Of course." She took his offered hand and stepped off the sled. *This is more like it!* Excitement built up in her at the very idea of running free. The past few hours had been far too long with too much time to think and ponder. Leaving a cache on the side of the trail for others to find and utilize, to allow the dog team to finish the trip quicker and easier — that made the most sense.

She stripped off all her clothing, ignoring the lustful looks her human form brought, before she opened the portal and shifted to wolf. This time was far easier than the first and she relished the control that understanding brought.

Soon they were off again, Alessandro staying human and directing the team, she and Maximus both changed to wolves and loping alongside. The dogs were far less fearful of them than they had been of the Ribelles, seeming to understand they were on the same side. Either that, or the Luceres were amazing dog-whisperers.

When they made the outskirts of town just after midnight dark as the midday, they stopped to re-dress. The interval had refreshed her, swept away the concerns and worries she had as human. She lingered at the side of the sled, reluctant to shift back to human. Her life felt so much simpler as wolf, far more straightforward. Of course, she would stay with her mates, that was so obvious in her animal form. Why did her wolf see so clearly, but her human side made such a big deal of everything? She had to share with the brothers her longing for the simpler life. "*I wish I could stay as wolf. It's the best. Everything is so much easier.*"

"*You can't do that all the time, unless you want never to be human again. Your wolf nature can take you over completely and not let you shift back, but then you'd never*" *experience the joys being human can bring, like raising your children in comfort and security. The wild animal, it's far more of a crap shoot, to steal a metaphor from your card counting days. Wolf pups are not guaranteed such luxuries in the wild."*

"You *think I'll never do that again? Counting cards is in my blood. I have a reputation to maintain as The Chameleon after all."* She teased Maximus who had answered her inquiry, ignoring the pangs of longing his words of caution brought. She dutifully shifted back to human and pulled on the offending clothes, ignoring his look of smoldering intensity.

"We'll soon have you safe and sound in your own bed, Trinity," Alessandro said quickly to fill the void. She glanced at him, but he was careful not to add any sexual inflection to his words. *Wise man.* She indeed wanted time alone to scrub off the past few days. God, a hot shower was going to be so freakin' heavenly!

Twenty minutes later, they dropped her off at the inn.

"We'll take care of the dogs and be right back," Alessandro said, but not before escorting her up to her rooms to check all was safe and secure.

"Thanks. I'll see you both in the morning. I need a hot shower, food and sleep," she mumbled before closing the door on the hurt that flashed briefly in his brown eyes. She desperately needed time away from the pair who tugged at her on every level, making thinking straight near impossible.

She dropped her clothing in a messy pile and ran to the bathroom, turning on the shower and cranking it up to its hottest setting. Long minutes spent under the pulsating heat of the massaging powerhead cleansed her flesh of the past few days, but did nothing for the erotic images that constantly assaulted her brain. Was this what addiction was like for the drug addict? An urge so powerful that it was all she could manage not to run after the Luceres brothers and throw herself on their mercy? Beg them to fuck her?

Was this a test? She turned off the water and grabbed a bath towel, pulling it tight around her before stepping out of the tub. Wiping the steam from the mirror over the sink, she gave a loud sigh of frustration at the woman with desperate eyes she was faced with.

"Goddamn it all to hell! This is my body! I say what happens to it, nobody else." Visions of the two brothers fighting for her, endangering themselves with the Ribelle bastards to keep her safe, replaced the sensual ones. The uplifting moment of their vowing to be the three musketeers. All the supportive and lovely things the pair of men had spoken to her these past few days. How wonderfully they had cared for her. It added up to so damn much.

"*Un pour tous, tous pour un.* One for all, all for one," she whispered at the woman in the mirror. Such perfect words. Such perfect men for her. *A lifetime spent in their company, would that be so difficult? Just a little marking and claiming and it's done. Together forever,* the pro-Luceres side of her brain asked.

She rubbed her forehead, trying to stop the onslaught. "Tomorrow, okay? Give me one night of peace, for heaven's sake."

Who else is there to run with that would understand a she-wolf?

Apparently, her deeper self wanted this settled *now.* She began to laugh hysterically, a meltdown too close for comfort. The laughter turned to tears. Her body shaking with sobs, she allowed herself the luxury of letting it all out just this once. The constant worries about her family, the twists and turns of her current life, the near-death experience she had just undergone. Finally cleansed, she stood straighter and looked herself right in the eye.

"What do *you* want, Trinity Wells?"

Her eyes shone with the knowledge of what she desired most deep in her heart.

"Then you shall have it," she promised the woman with the cornflower-blue eyes.

She pulled on a warm flannel nightgown and raided the small mini bar, pulling out little bottles of liquor, a huge bar of semi-sweet chocolate filled with nuts and raisins, and numerous salty snacks, then settled down cross-legged on the bed to savor the indulgence. She downed the cream liqueur in one satisfying gulp.

Then she attacked all the salty snacks with glee, tearing bags open. Having been told of her need for lots of calories and not much chance of weight gain only made the feast that much more fun. It was good to be wolf!

When her appetite finally abated, she washed her hands and brushed her teeth, then settled down to sleep. She had a huge day ahead and needed rest.

Sometime during the night, she woke, a slight sense of movement making her instantly alert. *What was that?* She didn't stir a muscle, but waited for her eyes to adjust to the dimness to avoid drawing attention to the fact that she was aware of a presence. A huge shape came into focus before settling down on a chair across the room. The awesome fragrance of soap and musk told the unmistakable tale.

She sat up straighter. "What are you doing here?" The distant sounds of wolves howling gave her a bad sense of déjà vu.

"I had to check on you—to make sure you're all right," Alessandro said, his voice low and growly, like it was not so easy to keep himself in check. If he thought that was bad, just breathing in his essence was affecting her on the most elemental level.

"I'm fine. What time is it?"

"Just after five. We sensed a threat and Maximus is checking into it. I came to keep you safe."

"Is this what it's going to be like? My assumed availability giving license to other wolves to think I'm up for grabs?" This insaneness had to end. No way did she want her best buds in dire danger due to her very existence.

He nodded. "Yes. Until we finish the ceremony, this is going to happen. I know it's unfortunate, and I would change it if I could for you. But I didn't make the damn rules." He hesitated and it was obvious he'd left something unsaid. His face had become clearer in the dimness as her eyes adjusted. She registered pain in his expression, especially his eyes that mirrored his sensitive soul that he normally kept hidden. "I heard you crying last night. It...affected me greatly. Is there anything I can do to help you?"

"Yes, as a matter of fact there is. Can you call Maximus? I want to talk to the both of you at the same time."

"Of course." She heard him seek out his twin using telepathy.

She gathered all her resources for the coming conversation, telling herself it was all going to work out just fine. It had to.

The silence between them stretched as they waited for Maximus to join them. Then he was coming through the door with an inquisitive expression on his handsome mug. He looked like a man in charge, not at all worried by another threat. She breathed a sigh of relief. No way was one of these amazing men going to be accosted again if she had any say in it.

He came close and leaned down to give her a kiss, his eyes alight with an intensity that suggested how happy he was to see her. And how happy he would be to be with her. *Anytime.* No surprise there—the two men were as virile as they came. *And then some.*

"Morning, *tesoro.* You're looking lovely as always." His lips captured hers and she wanted nothing more than to get right down to enjoying everything he and his brother offered, but this was a time for clearer heads.

"Have a seat. I want to talk to the two of you and having you this close—well, it makes it difficult to think straight."

She was rewarded with a wolfish grin that said he knew *exactly* how much she wanted them, before he dropped his large body into a chair next to Alessandro.

"This putting the two of you in danger has got to stop."

"Don't be worried. We've got this," Maximus said with decidedly alpha directness.

"All humans have approximately fifty trillion single cells. And apparently, all of mine have decided you two are the one for me." She shook her head at the idea.

"Then we are decided," Maximus said, a gleam in his eye saying he was one second away from marking and claiming her.

She put up a hand. "No, stop right there! You need to listen to what I have to say. Nothing has been decided yet. I need to know more."

"What do you need, Trinity?" Alessandro asked. His concern was expressed clearly in his deep brown eyes and furrowed forehead.

"Well, for one thing, I need assurances that I can go ahead with my teaching career. That I can continue to live in Rome during the semester and fulfill my contract with the university. Otherwise—" She waved her hand around. "None of this is going to happen. I won't leave one situation just to fall into another that's just as restrictive."

"You're talking about your family controlling your life. Right?" Alessandro asked. He leaned forward in his chair. His extreme interest flattered her and she rose to the occasion.

"Well, yes, I don't want that same thing to happen all over again. You guys, you're so alpha that it scares me." As much as she hated to admit it, it was the truth. This was not the time to avoid saying it exactly as it was for her. This was the time to step up and ensure the best future possible.

"We don't want you to ever feel frightened around us. We'd *never* ask more of you than you can give. It's not a one-way street with us doing all the taking, Trinity. It's you letting us know what you need and we will be there to provide it. Of course, you should fulfill your contract. We enjoy researching at the University of Sapienza. Their archives are very helpful to our understanding of Roman history. The Lupus Sanguis Chalice is not the only artifact we seek."

The well-chosen words were a calming balm. She nodded her approval. "Yes, that's what I needed to hear from you. You agree with all this, Maximus? What Alessandro has said?"

His expression was smoldering before he gave a slight nod. "Yes, I want our mate to be happy, as much as Alessandro does." He looked her straight in the eyes to let her see the truth. "And if it means giving her — you — full rein to keep you fulfilled, so be it."

She let an audible breath out. "All right. Okay, then, I think I'm ready."

"Do you mean what I think you mean?" Alessandro asked.

"There are moments in life when what comes after is entirely different that what came before — life-changing moments. This week, meeting and being with you both, it's been entirely life changing for me. We've experienced a rare connection — an honest connection, as real as it gets. A benchmark of what our lives can be to one another. I don't *ever* want the pair of you in any danger. I mean, you both saved my life and I can never thank you enough for that. And of my being unclaimed or unmarked, or whatever the impediment to giving us the opportunity for a happy future, I don't want it standing in our way."

"But what about how you feel about us? We both know how we feel about you."

Maximus nodded his head at his brother's words.

"I've never felt more alive in my life since I've met you two. Sure, it overwhelms me at times, the feelings that the two of you are stirring inside me. But it's also been the best time and I can't imagine my life without the both of you in it." She threw back the covers and relished the changing expressions on the twins' faces as they instantly recognised her invitation.

The pair advanced toward her, two powerful predators preparing to take their mate. She gulped. *What have I done?* But there was no going back now.

"How do we do this?" she asked, hearing the trembling worry underlying her tone. *Duh!* She'd never been more nervous in her freakin' life.

Chapter Twenty-Seven

Trinity

"It's simple really. But it hurts less if we are making love when we do it," Alessandro explained. He began removing his clothing in an orderly fashion. Maximus yanked his own off so violently that buttons broke and flew around the room, pinging like gunshots on the floor as he made himself naked in a split second.

Aww, the beauty of the two ancient-appearing warriors as they stood naked by her bedside. She took a deep breath. The sex, that was going to be the best part. The marking, not so much.

"Let me get this thing off you," Maximus said, tugging her nightgown up and over her head before she could object. His eyes smoldered as he looked at her naked breasts. She kept her hands down at her side, enjoying the power his interest aroused in her. She even preened a little. It was good to be so hugely desired, like he wanted to ravish every square inch of her body.

"So beautiful," he murmured, reaching out a hand. Alessandro did the same from the other side and both men caressed her, making her feel faint with arousal. When Maximus took a pebbled nipple into his warm mouth and sucked hard on it, she moaned. Her pussy fluttered and squeezed in painful waves of urgent need, desperate to have a cock or cocks to push inside and stretch her to glorious fulfillment. Did that make her unusual or odd? Who cared? It was right for her. And obviously right for her mates.

She stretched out a hand to each of them, grabbing hold of two very fine cocks and eliciting a deep moan from each throat.

"Do we have to be connected in a specific way for the ceremony?" she asked. She used her fingers to squeeze and test the plush firmness of their fully erect cocks enjoying the moment of control. Not that it would be a hardship for the two alphas to gain entry to her body at the same time. Considering the enticing idea made wetness gush and heat flash through her body.

"Yes, but have you heard the term *knotting*?"

She shook her head. "No. What is it?"

The two brothers exchanged a pointed look.

"Okay, share," she demanded.

"Our cocks have an extra—*ahem*—feature," Alessandro said with pride. The smug expression on Maximus' face confirmed his assessment.

"How do you mean? Sure, they're incredibly fine, but they look normal to me," she said, surprised by his words.

"When a wolf or wolves claim their mate, they swell up inside the female to the extent that their bodies are locked together for the duration of the lovemaking,"

Alessandro explained, his eyes alight with a certain fire echoed in his brother's expression.

"Ahh, why?" The concept mind-boggled, though it did explain the incredible sensations.

"It's just how things are. Nature's way of cementing and binding the relationship, I would imagine," Alessandro said.

"Does it ever hurt?"

"Not if you're fully aroused and that's the only way it will ever happen between us." Alessandro tweaked and played with her nipple as he explained, his touch increasing her arousal.

"So how do we do this thing?" She was impatient now to get on with the enjoyment their bodies would bring.

"Well, we have to go one at a time. No woman can take two knots at the same time."

"Who goes first?" she asked. No way was she going to decide and cause a possible rift between the brothers.

"We claim and mark you at the same time — twice," Maximus growled with impatience.

She startled. "I thought that was impossible?" She suddenly wanted to flee. If they thought she was going to allow two cocks to swell up so large inside her that she was trapped between them, they had another think coming.

"No, he means that only one of us needs to be inside you when we do the honors before switching and doing it a second time."

"Okay." She nodded her head, relieved at the sensible explanation. The need to be taken had became stronger in the past few minutes, her body desperate, knowing the pleasure that awaited. A pleasure like no other, judging by the last time they had all been together.

"Before we begin, we need to say the words," Alessandro warned. "Once we do this thing, it cannot be undone. Do you accept us, Trinity Wells, as your Forever Mates? Maximus and Alessandro of the House of Luceres?"

His words touched her on an elemental level. Could she bind herself to these two men in such a permanent way? She swallowed hard, her heart beating so loudly she could hear it echoing inside her head. There would be no going back from this. No divorce. Just guaranteed companionship and excellent lovemaking for all time. *Yes!* She could do this and she would embrace it.

"I, Trinity Wells, accept you Maximus and Alessandro of the House of Luceres as my Forever Mates. I promise to be true to you for all of my days."

"I, Maximus of House of Luceres, accept you, Trinity Wells, as my Forever Mate. Now let's get on with it!" Maximus growled.

Maximus tugged her toward him. He pushed her legs wide open with his hands and pressed his mouth against her pussy, running his gloriously raspy and talented tongue up her channel, sweeping it back and forth before seeking entrance and plunging inside, making her gasp aloud.

"You like, *tesoro*?" he murmured before clamping down on her clit and teasing it with his lips. It was too much and she began to spiral into orgasm.

"Please, I need your cock. *Now*," she said, her voice trembling with emotion.

He wrapped his hands in her hair, and keeping a tight grip, he pushed himself deep inside her. Each long stroke of his huge cock centered all her attention on how fucking great it felt to be filled by him, stretched by him, easing the terrible ache within. Alessandro caressed her breasts from behind, tugging at her nipples causing even more wetness to spill from her as he trailed kisses along the side of her neck.

When the base of Maximus' length began swelling inside her pussy, the erotic pressure forced a cry from her, the nearly fist-sized knot rubbing against nerves locked deep inside that screamed from the attention.

"Oh *yes*, fuck me! Harder!" she demanded, her body taking complete control. Her mind refused now to worry about how she sounded or acted, the sensation too great for her to ever want to escape their clutches. *Give me more.* She was vibrating, her body rocked to the core with waves of indescribable pleasure.

She surrendered to her raging instincts, the need to be fucked totally by her warriors. She understood the heat now, how it enabled the greatest ecstasy the body could imagine.

"Sweet, tight pussy," Maximus crooned. "So wet, so needy. Take it all."

She was so tightly clenched around him now, her cunt so swollen, so locked onto him, that she lost all sense of time. It was just them and her, pushing her body to ever more increasing heights of passion.

At the pinnacle of pleasure, when they were all maddened by the sights, the fragrance, the very audaciousness of the sensations abounding between them, he leaned forward and bit down on her shoulder just as his brother did the same on the other side.

Brief pain followed by a soothing warmth as they both licked the wounds with their hot tongues, exciting her flesh further.

"My turn," Alessandro growled as his brother's cock finally released and he was able to ease out of her.

Alessandro instantly replaced Maximus, his cock iron-hard as he pushed himself into her slit and her still spasming pussy. The base of his cock became swollen almost immediately, and he pressed into flesh made sensitive by all the raw fucking. She embraced him, vibrating with acute need that had not been all spent with his brother. Her body knew exactly what to do, embracing the stretching and pounding once more with wild abandon.

His brother reached down between them and massaged her clit, making her mewl as her body allowed even more intrusion of Alessandro's pulsating member. He spurted cum into her, filling her to overflowing.

"She is ours, brother, our beautiful Forever Mate is all ours."

"Yes, we will love and cherish her and keep her happy all the days of her life."

She could hear both men perfectly in her mind just before they bit down on her shoulders together for the final bites, a twin action that hurt before it was eased by eager tongues. *Tongues that will be put to even more excellent use in the future,* she promised herself as she rode Alessandro's knot, the stretching almost beyond endurance, yet so intensely exhilarating. For long moments of time, riding the ultimate rapture a human being could endure, she could forget everything else. *Be one with my Forever Mates.*

She fell asleep some time later, cocooned between them, their limbs intertwined. When morning came, again without the sunrise, she awoke and found herself the happiest, most contented she had ever been. Gazing down at her two alphas who embraced her, snuggled her protectively, she gave thanks for the beginning of her new life, a journey she could not have imagined entering upon only a few days ago. But now, it meant everything to her.

Home would be wherever they were. They had gifted her with amazing power to change the world, for the good, and a sense of being chosen by destiny.

And it did not get any better than that.

Want to see more from this author? Here's a taster for you to enjoy!

Sin City Wolf: Honor
January Bain

Coming February 2022

Excerpt

Lucius

"Look! There's a halo around the moon tonight, Lucius. You know what that means?" Veronica purred. Her mouth was coated in far too much red lipstick for my liking, though I more than appreciated her luscious body and adventurous spirit.

"What do you think it means?" I asked, not particularly interested in her take on it. I couldn't imagine the notorious party girl having done much digging into mythology or history. If I wanted facts, my twin brothers Maximus and Alexandro would be the ones I'd call on. One of the things I did like about Veronica's type though—easy to forget. I didn't need any complications as enforcer for the House of Luceres beyond those necessary to protect my pack.

"It means something momentous is on its way."

She looked up at me, her eyes huge, reflecting not only the light of the roaring bonfire kept alight for the entirety of the Lupercalia festival, but I swear I caught a glimpse of myself in them too, in all my tall, dark and Luceres glory. Our lineage was blessed with good genetics and lots of money, and my role in it demanded I exercise and stay in shape.

"Wait, what did you say? That something's coming?" Her words caught up with me.

"Could be good. Or evil. It depends on the intentions of the spirit." Veronica shivered for effect in a dress that barely covered essentials. Her unexpected announcement was suddenly accompanied by the howling of a lone wolf in the distance. I went on high alert. In the desert, on a clear night such as this, sound was deceiving. The interloper could be miles away...or nearby.

I glanced around the firepit, checking out the pack members milling about. Emily, one of the cousins, was dancing with wild abandon. I frowned. Wasn't she a bit young for this? The festival was notorious for events that would curl a human's hair. Rumors abounded and things that probably should not happen...happened. Case in point, headed right toward me was a former one-night stand, her finger pointed at me like she had something to say, something I was certain I would prefer not to hear. What was her name again? *Serena, Simona, Sawyer...*

Before it came to me, she was right in my face. "Lucius Luceres, I got some...thing to say to you you're not go...ing to like." She poked at me with a pointy red fingernail, her words slurring and her body language suggesting something vastly different.

"Step back, if you know what's good for you, cur!" Veronica yelled at her.

"What you go...ing to do about it?"

Right, *Simone*, one of the more jealous ones. Why was one night never enough for them? *Not like I ever promise anything more.* I stepped back. Let them have at it. A gorgeous female standing farther from the fire winked at me, her eyes taking in the foolish provocation with obvious interest. I gave her my patented cool-billionaire smile.

She replied with an air kiss, pulling me forward with all the magnetic pull of true north. Just the way I like it. And man, those curves, highlighted in a tight dress that left nothing to the imagination.

"Hey, where are you going?" Veronica quickly noticed my mental desertion, soon to be followed by a physical one.

I turned back and sighed. The two women had each other by the hair. Soon they'd shift, by the look of things. I didn't want the hassle, but after all, I had caused it, even though they'd both been warned that I never dated.

"Come on, ladies, the festival is almost over. Wouldn't you rather be having fun than fighting?"

"This is fun! I'm going to beat her ass!" And with that Veronica shed her clothes and shifted, one second vanishing through the otherworldly portal in a shimmer of light, and in the next back again as a blue-eyed gray wolf. It had been explained to me by my scholarly brothers that the dimension is only one of eleven that create the multiverse. *Whatever.* I was just satisfied it worked.

I mean, who doesn't want to be wolf?

One second later, Simone followed Veronica, her leaner and meaner wolf appearing in a flash of light. Of course, she was the more perturbed of the two, giving her the edge. The pair squared off. Simone growled as she lowered her head to bully her opponent, the thick ruff on her spine fully erect.

Instantly, others picked up on the change of energy. Bodies began streaming in from everywhere, surrounding the two females in mere seconds. This was what the pack wanted. *Craved.* The music shifted, became a louder drumbeat that stirred the blood.

I threw a nonchalant shrug to the gorgeous female watching the antics from the sidelines as if to say, *what can I do? Females will be females.* She rolled her eyes.

Turning back to the action, I decided not to intervene in the fight, not unless they began to inflict real damage. These kinds of fights could be more about posturing than anything else, useful for ratcheting down minor disagreements and aggressions, the reason this festival was held in the first place. It allowed pack members time to listen to their wolf, step away from the imposing limits of civilization. *Freedom, baby.*

But I had apparently misjudged the level of anger and animosity between the pair. Claws and fur flying, they lunged at each other, rolling in the desert sand and sending a blanket of dust into the air.

The crowd roared their approval. Someone had appointed themselves the holder of the bets and numbers were being tossed around the ring like confetti. Eager faces were alight with the excitement I'd imagine common to the Colosseum of ancient days, and they began to holler loudly for their favorite.

It seemed that Simone was holding sway, her anger the most apparent to the catcalling crew. Hell, half of them were undressing now, probably looking to take a turn.

Great, a bloom of blood had appeared on Veronica's fur. Now I had to shift. Not really a bad thing as I love to be wolf. The power, the freedom, the pure sense of being removed from this world…it didn't get any better.

I removed my clothing, knowing the new female was checking me out. *Have at it. I'm choice.* I jumped into the fray and in seconds, had Veronica by the scruff of the neck, subjecting her to dominance, forcing her to give over to her alpha. She whined, then lay down. Simone stood on four stiffened paws, her tongue lolling, still defying me.

I flew at her, catching her by the throat, taking her down to the ground. It wasn't hard enough to break the skin, but enough to inflict some pain. She needed to learn her place.

When she gave me proper respect, I let her slink away, then shifted and redressed. The interested female was still watching and I nodded at her. She sauntered over, her spectacular hips swaying to the rhythmic beat of the snare drum one of the pack members was pounding on, her smile coy.

The crowd clapped and stamped their feet loudly, naked breasts bouncing to the delight of the males who watched with approval, obviously having enjoyed the show. Money was exchanged and backs were slapped. Just another night at the Lupercalia. And mild compared to some events I won't get into.

"Nice moves," she said, getting closer enough to pick an imaginary piece of lint from my jacket.

"I aim to please."

"I take it you're not worried that a rare witch moon is causing chaos this night?" The new female pointed at the night sky. A dark cloud was now creeping across the luminous surface, lending an even more eerie appearance to proceedings.

"Witch moon? Where did you hear that?" A cold finger traced my spine. I shook the odd sensation off. *An old wives' tale.*

"Big strong wolf like you—you have nothing to fear."

Never trust a witch.

The warning from an elderly Italian relative came to mind. Well, not like I had any in my pack or knew of any in my round of acquaintances. And I certainly wouldn't bed one. Now, the wolf throwing herself at me at the moment, sure.

I'm partial to blondes and easy tail...

* * * *

Isadora

I placed an arm around Elena's thin shoulders, my heart breaking for my younger sister who was the mirror image of me with her smooth fall of titian hair, legs that didn't quit and a bod that drew more than her fair share of attention. But she didn't look like a goddess at the moment. I'd never seen her this upset, not even when her first boyfriend had dropped her just before prom...though it was fun enacting a spell to cause him to grow horns and a tail for the event.

Of course, I wouldn't do anything like that again. If I'd learned anything, it was cost of being rash in such endeavors. *Everything one does has a karma attached to it, like it or not. Good deeds attract good energy.*

It was the way of the witch—or a good witch, which is what I considered myself. Okay, I had to work on it at times. *Nobody's perfect, right?* But hell yeah, I tried to stay in the good-witch zone.

Elena turned her tear-stained face toward me. I swore she'd lost weight in the past few days. Was she even eating?

"I know I was stupid to care so much. But he was so kind to me, so handsome and romantic. I thought we'd made a real connection. I wouldn't have gone with him otherwise. You know that, right? I'm not easy. I've only been with a few guys."

I rubbed her back. "He's a damn fool. And no, you're definitely not easy. You're the best he could ever imagine being with. It's his loss."

"I should have known better. He's too good for me, being a Luceres and all."

My ire heated. "You're as good as any Luceres. In fact, this proves you're better."

"Then why didn't he think so?"

My stomach squeezed into a fist. "Which Luceres was it? I've got an idea. We're not going to let him get away with this."

Elena sat up straighter, a bit of hope in her teary eyes. "It was Lucius Luceres from the Glitter Palace. What are you going to do? Make him come back to me?"

"Sorry, sweetheart, that I can't do, not without doing something we'd both be sorry for. That kind of action comes with a steep cost. But damn it, I can make him pay!"

"Okay. That's something at least." I caught an odd look in her eyes, like she was trying to decide something. Maybe her tender heart was saying not to harm the guy who she'd once admired? No way would my sister try to deceive me. She didn't have it in her.

"But I should tell you, we didn't *actually* go all the way. Lots of kissing and hugging though. But the connection, I swear it was there. You believe me, right?"

I nodded, though I'd assumed they'd gone further, had made love all night long. "Of course, sweetheart. Promises can be made without actual sex."

"What do you want me to do?" Elena pressed onward.

At least Elena's tears had dried up. I gave my options a quick perusal. "I think he needs a taste of his own medicine. And I think we'll do this by calling on the power of the coven. Lots of them were done wrong by men. Why not let them be the catalyst for inflicting a fair revenge?" I relished the quick look of interest that instantly appeared on my sister's lovely face at this idea.

"*Ooh*, that could work! You'd do that for me?"

"Of course, sweetheart." There was nothing I wouldn't do for my family. I'd even picked up the heaviest debt of all, one that I would take on again, if need be, though the cost was beyond belief. I'd be enslaved to the end of my days. But that didn't bear thinking about now. I had something I could do to help my sister — though spells weren't really my thing — but it wouldn't cost too much if I chose wisely and avoided the evil one. *Shouldn't. Hopefully...*

"Can I watch?" she asked.

"No, it's best you don't get involved. Let me bear the fallout." *And it's not like I haven't had lots of practice.*

She looked disappointed, then gave in. "Okay, as long as he pays."

My sister scurried off and I set to work, first lining up photos of my coven in a nice precise row. Twelve in all, me being the thirteenth. I didn't want to bother them for this undertaking that I could easily handle myself. Most of my sisters of another mother had such busy lives...and they wouldn't be very happy with what I was doing. But photos captured the spirit at a moment in time, giving images energy that could be used for future events, so they'd do.

I turned next to my gleaming array of crystals, my green glass containers of hard-to-find ingredients as they all had to be handpicked and ground by mortar and pestle and my vials of shimmering liquids that moved of their own accord, catching the light as they bubbled and swirled.

Hmm, how far do I want to carry this? For Elena — hell, for all those harmed by the notorious womanizer — nothing was more important than stopping the wolf dead in his tracks. A devious plan suddenly formed in my mind.

Well, well, wolf, by the hair on my chinny chin-chin, you'd better look out, for here I come...and guess what? You won't...

Home of Erotic Romance

Sign up for our newsletter and find out about all our romance book releases, eBook sales and promotions, sneak peeks and FREE romance books!

About the Author

January Bain has wished on every falling star, every blown-out birthday candle and every coin thrown in a fountain to be a storyteller. To share the tales of high adventure, mysteries, and full-blown thrillers she has dreamed of all her life. The story you now have in your hands is the compilation of a lot of things manifesting itself for this special series. Hundreds of hours spent researching the unusual and the mundane have come together to create a series that features strong women who don't take life too seriously, wild adventures full of twists and unforeseen turns, and hot complicated men who aren't afraid to take risks. She can only hope the stories of her beloved Brass Ringers will capture your imagination as much as they did hers when she wrote them.

If you are looking for January Bain, you can find her hard at work every morning without fail in her office with two furry babies trying to prove who does a better job of guarding the doorway. And, of course, she's married to the most romantic man! Who once famously replied to her inquiry about buying fresh flowers for their home every week, "Give me one good reason why not?" Leaving her speechless and knocking her head against the proverbial wall for being so darn foolish. She loves flowers.

January loves to hear from readers. You can find her contact information, website details and author profile page at https://www.totallybound.com